A Fighting Chance

by

Chrys Fey

Disaster Crimes, Book 6

This is a work of fiction. Names, characters, places, and incidents are either the product of the author's imagination or are used fictitiously, and any resemblance to actual persons living or dead, business establishments, events, or locales, is entirely coincidental.

A Fighting Chance

Contact Information: info@thewildrosepress.com

Cover Art by *Kim Mendoza*

The Wild Rose Press, Inc.
PO Box 708
Adams Basin, NY 14410-0708
Visit us at www.thewildrosepress.com

Publishing History
First Crimson Rose Edition, 2021
Trade Paperback ISBN 978-1-5092-3441-7
Digital ISBN 978-1-5092-3442-4

Disaster Crimes, Book 6
Published in the United States of America

Dedication

To everyone who loves Thorn
and wants to see him get
his much-deserved happy ending.
~
To all domestic abuse and sexual assault survivors.
You are HEROINES OF STEEL!

Acknowledgments

A HUGE thanks to The Wild Rose Press, Lori Graham (my editor), Kim Mendoza (my cover artist), and Bill Nevitt (my audio book narrator) for sticking with me through the completion of the Disaster Crimes series.

Chapter One

Thorn walked into The Fighting Chance, a self-defense studio. A few times a week, he made it a point to stop in to visit with his best friend who owned the studio, Beth Goldwyn; to spend time with his twin god kids; and to check on Amanda, the woman he thought about every day. Amanda was Beth's assistant, a survivor of domestic violence. No, she was a warrior. Thorn didn't know exactly what her ex-boyfriend had done to her, but Beth told him it was bad. He didn't know if Amanda would ever tell him. Or if she'd ever let him get closer to her.

Last Christmas, they'd had a moment he often replayed in his mind at night when he couldn't fall asleep. They'd danced in each other's arms, and then they had shared a kiss beneath the mistletoe. That kiss had stunned him, because it had been Amanda's idea, and when he was about to stop before their lips could touch, she had closed the distance. To touch her like that had nearly knocked him off his feet.

Touch. For a long time, Amanda had been afraid to let anyone touch her. It had taken her years before she threw her arms around Beth, hugging her. Shortly after that, she shook Thorn's hand, something Beth said was a miracle. To not want to be touched, Thorn could only speculate over what Amanda had endured at the hands of her ex, which caused anger to boil inside him. So, he tried not to think about it, but Beth hinted Amanda was scarred mentally and physically. Thorn hadn't so much as caught a glimpse of a scar, but if she had one, or more, she was keeping them well hidden. He wanted to see them. Touch them. Kiss them.

Touch…kiss…they'd done both before, but Thorn started to doubt they'd ever do them again. Since Christmas, Amanda had taken several steps back from him. Figuratively speaking.

Last month, the twins were baptized. Amanda had worn a beautiful white dress. He busted out dress pants and looped the lavender tie from Beth and Donovan's wedding around his neck, much to Beth's delight. Amanda held Reagan, and he held Ryan, as godmother and godfather. Thorn's heart pounded the entire time, not because he was in front of a church full of people, but because he stood so close to Amanda, touching. Their gazes connected as they held the babies over the basin. The moment was intimate in a way that startled him. Afterward, he escaped with a lie of being called in to work. In truth, he couldn't stay there any longer, not knowing he wouldn't be able to be that close to Amanda again, not with the things he felt inside. And still, he came to The Fighting Chance several times a week. Did he have a fighting chance in regard to Amanda? Would he have a relationship with her one day?

God, he hoped so.

He arrived during their lunch break, the perfect time to chase Reagan and Ryan over the blue mat, as they crawled away to escape him, and to talk to Amanda. She stood behind the receptionist's desk, eating a salad and drinking from a bottle of water.

When he came in, she dropped the fork with spinach leaves and a slice of cucumber speared on the prongs. She brushed off her hands and shifted in place. Nervous reactions. She had them every time he was around. He didn't know if it was from her history of abuse or if it was from attraction. He hoped for the latter.

"Hey, Amanda."

"Hey."

She avoided eye contact, so he went around the counter to where the twins stood in their bouncers, knowing she needed a minute. He squatted in front of them. "Hey, kids." He ruffled Ryan's hair. Then he rubbed his fingers over Reagan's cheek. They bounced on their little feet, excited to see him. He played with them, pushing the buttons on their bouncers and flicking the toys. Everything he did delighted them.

Out of the corner of his eye, he noticed Amanda seated on the stool behind the counter, watching him interact with the twins.

"Have the two of you been good for Auntie Amanda?" He turned toward her.

She smiled. "Yes, they have been. They're perfect. Beth and Donovan won the lottery with these two."

"They certainly did." He stood. "How have you been?"

She rubbed her hands between her knees. "Good. I've been good."

He didn't want to say her ex's name, but the bastard was out there. Somewhere. He had made it known with a note that said "found you." Other notes followed that one—"you can't escape me," "you're mine," "I'm not going anywhere," and "I'll have you again."

That last one had sent lava through Thorn's veins. That was what Amanda was the most afraid of—that he'd get her and do his worse.

It'd been weeks since the last note. Another was due any day now.

Thorn nodded. "I'm glad." Relieved was more like it.

He slipped his hands into his pockets. "Look, I wanted to ask you…" Words failed him. He'd wanted to ask her for months but had chickened out each time.

She tilted her head when he paused. "Yes?"

He shook his head. "Never mind. It can wait."

Damn it, he thought to himself. *Stop being a wuss*!

Amanda got to her feet. She took a few steps toward him, but then she quickly took one step back. He kept his gaze lowered. When she lifted a hand to reach out to him, his heart palpitated. *Please.* He sent the plea silently to Amanda. *Please do something so I know…so I won't be such a coward. Please, Amanda…*

She dropped her hand to her side.

He looked at her.

Her chest rose and fell as if she were breathless. She opened her mouth, and a pent-up breath fled from her lips. Her mouth opened wider, as if to speak, but—

Beth's voice called out from her office at the back of the studio. "Amanda, can you help me for a second?"

Amanda stared into Thorn's eyes with lowered brows. She looked sad, and he felt like an idiot for not having the guts to ask what he'd been dying to ask her. If he didn't have it in him, how could he expect her to? He gave her a small nod, letting her know it was okay to leave. She moved past him. When she did, the backs of their hands brushed. He blinked, surprised.

Not daring to move, he listened to the sound of her shoes when she went to the back.

Something cracked into his kneecap.

"Ow."

Reagan's toy rattle lay on the ground next to him. He shifted to see her standing in the bouncer, with her hand on her hip and her small, round face scrunched up in a glare that clearly said, "You're such an idiot."

"You do take after your mom," he muttered.

Beside her, Ryan tilted his head back and let out baby giggles that reminded him too much of Donovan making fun of him.

"And you're just like your dad."

He bent down and picked up the rattle. "Promise to not hit me in the head?"

Reagan eyed him.

Skeptical, he gave the rattle back to her.

She took it and bashed it on her bouncer a couple of times, not taking her glare off him.

"What did I do?" he asked.

She let out a huff.

"Okay, so I screwed up." He glanced toward the hallway. "What should I do?"

Ryan leaned forward and babbled something in baby language. Reagan turned to him and shot back a string of gibberish. She lifted her left hand and moved it from side to side, signaling Ryan to let her handle this. Ryan leaned back against his bouncer, as if to say, "Okay. This will be entertaining."

Thorn gaped. "My God, you really are like your parents."

Ryan burst into giggles again.

Reagan shook the rattle urgently to shut him up.

Then she pointed the rattle at Thorn and went into a long speech that he couldn't understand, and yet…he could. He nodded when she went quiet. "I'll do my best. I promise."

A smile bloomed on her face, and she let out a happy squeal.

"What was all that about?"

Thorn looked to see Amanda standing a few feet away.

He pushed to his feet. "It's a secret."

That had her smiling. "You're cute with them."

"They're the cute ones. They make me look good." He moved to his place on the other side of the counter, giving her the space to go to her place behind the desk. "Um." He took a deep breath. "Would you like to go out with me some time? For dinner?"

Amanda's eyelids popped open wide.

"Or…or lunch?"

She still didn't respond.

"Brunch? No. Not brunch. Who goes to brunch? Coffee? Or if you don't like coffee…water. We can get water." He winced inwardly. *Did I ask her out to get water?* He wanted to smack himself. Who does that?

Apparently, he does.

"You can think about it and let me know…sometime." He glanced once more at her face. Her eyes were wide, her mouth parted slightly, and he wasn't sure if the blood had drained from her face or not, but she appeared paler. Part of him wanted to apologize. Had he overstepped? Was he way out of line thinking she felt something for him?

He turned to leave. That would be the last time he ever listened to a baby.

"Wait…" Amanda reached over the counter to stop him. "I…" She straightened. "I would like that."

He stared at her a second, dumbfounded. "Uh. Which one?"

She smiled. "Coffee. Tomorrow? Before work?"

Thorn's heart soared. "I can pick you up."

"No…I like to have my car with me." She paused to stare down at her hands, and he understood right then that her car was a safety precaution—a way out, in case Damon ever came around.

She peered back up at him. "Text me where, and I'll be there."

They stared at each other a moment.

"Bye, Amanda."

"Bye. See you tomorrow."

Thorn went to his car feeling on top of the world. *Finally*, he thought.

Finally.

Chapter Two

Amanda couldn't believe she'd agreed to have coffee with Thorn. She wanted to have coffee with him. And lunch. And dinner. Heck, she'd have brunch with him. But she never thought she'd actually do it. That she'd have the guts. Part of her was thrilled at the idea, but the other part of her was terrified. There was a reason why she'd kept him at arm's length, or farther, all this time. To keep him safe.

She stared at the text Thorn had sent her of the spot they were supposed to meet for coffee. In her other hand, she gripped her car keys. She should be leaving to meet him on time, but her feet were rooted to the spot. A dozen thoughts ran through her mind. She could tell him something came up and she couldn't meet him. She could stand him up. No. She couldn't do that to him. Grasping her phone and keys, she brought her hands to her forehead. Gosh, she hated herself. She hated her fear, her anxiety, her doubt, and everything that was making this harder than it should be. Thorn was an amazing man. He was sweet, gentle, nice, and protective—everything that Damon wasn't.

"No, no, don't think his name. Don't even think it." She stomped her foot and thrust her hands down in aggravation. One of Damon's powers was to get into her head. That's how he screwed up her life without even being present. His memory prevented her from following her dreams. His past torment paralyzed her in the present.

Well, he wasn't going to get in the way now. Nope. She marched for her door. Still, she looked through the peephole first, making sure he wasn't out there, waiting for her. Then, with her finger on the button of the pepper spray keychain, she made her way to her car. She checked the back seat before getting in and locking the door right away.

She followed Thorn's instructions to a park. Frowning, she pulled into the parking lot. She spotted him sitting on a bench near his car. He looked impossibly cute sitting there, grasping his hands and staring down at the grass and dirt, no doubt wondering if she would be coming or not. Swallowing down her nerves, she parked her car beside his and got out.

He popped to his feet. "Hey."

"Hi." She stepped onto the sidewalk. "Sorry I'm late."

"That's okay."

Inhaling the fresh green scent of a May morning in Florida, she gazed around. "Interesting place to come to for a cup of coffee."

He smiled. "There's a café-style food truck here. They make amazing coffee. Plus, I thought walking through the park would be more comfortable and less awkward than sitting at a table in some coffee shop."

She appreciated that more than she could say. The fact he considered her comfort level warmed her heart. "This is perfect."

Thorn led her to the food truck, and they ordered coffee. With their to-go cups of coffee in hand, they walked side by side through the park, following a path that brought them through trees and gardens. Birds chirped, and squirrels darted out of the path when they came near. They walked silently and doing so calmed Amanda.

Two butterflies danced into the path and fluttered around them. Laughing, Amanda stopped walking as the butterflies circled around their heads, trying to find each other. She ducked and bumped into Thorn, who put a hand on her shoulder. Finally, the butterflies flew past them and continued to fly chaotically in loops and spirals down the path. Amanda watched them until they disappeared around the curve.

"Welcome to Florida, where even butterflies can swarm," Thorn said.

She laughed. "I think we got in their way."

"I think so, too."

Smiling, Amanda started to walk again. "Have you always lived in Florida?"

He nodded. "Born and raised."

"And you've always been on the police force?"

"Yup. My father was a cop. He was one of the best men I knew, and I wanted to be just like him. He cared about everyone. Serve and protect wasn't merely his job, but his life, even out of his uniform. I try to live by that."

"You do."

He glanced at her.

She nodded.

He served and protected Beth, Donovan, and the twins. He served and protected the students at The Fighting Chance. And he served and protected her.

Taking a sip of coffee, she wondered what she should ask next. She hadn't exactly gone on many first dates outside of high school and college. In fact, Damon had been the last one.

"What about you?" Thorn asked. "Has Florida always been your home?"

"No. I moved here from North Carolina." She chewed on her bottom lip. Should she tell him why she had to move? Why she chose Florida?

Thorn saved her from saying more on that when he asked, "What jobs did you have before you decided to kick ass?"

She smiled at him, but that smile faded. This question would be harder to answer. "I was a first-grade teacher."

"Really?"

"Mm-hm. But you can't exactly be around little kids when you have bruises on your face."

Thorn's face became slack. He swallowed. "I'm sorry."

She licked her lips. "They asked me to resign so I could figure out what to do. They knew firing me wouldn't look good, so I quit. After that, I worked any job I could get to pay the bills. I was a cashier for a while, until customers started to look at me funny…because of my bruises. I cleaned hotel rooms for a long time, until a broken arm made that difficult." She peered down at the dirt path. "When I came here, I had a phone job because I was too scared to leave the house. I spent most of my time watching soap operas and surfing the Web. That's actually how I found the website for The Fighting Chance. I was searching self-defense techniques, and there it was. The first lesson I went to was the first time I actually got out of the house. Before then, I'd been paying for my groceries to be delivered." She took a deep breath, surprised she had revealed all that, but it was the tip of the iceberg.

"I'm glad you found The Fighting Chance," Thorn said, cutting into the silence.

She turned to him. "Me, too."

In that moment, she yearned to take his hand, to hold it, but she couldn't lift her arm to do it. So, she looked away at the nature surrounding them instead. It was a beautiful day. The sun was warm, the breeze cooling, and nature was alive with springtime.

They walked together. In a garden bursting with flowers, Amanda paused in front of a flowerbed full of daisies. A few bees buzzed from bloom to bloom. "Daisies are my favorite." She let out a sigh.

Thorn peered left and right. Then he stepped into the flower bed, plucked off a daisy, and hopped back onto the path. He held out the daisy to her.

"I'm pretty sure that's stealing," she said as she took it.

"It's okay. I'm a cop."

"Then you should know better." Grinning, she slipped the stem through the hole in the lid of her empty coffee cup. "It's pretty."

During the rest of their walk, she kept stealing peeks at it. Such a simple flower, such a simple gesture, and yet, they meant so much to her. Words got stuck in her throat, knotted up there with everything else she wanted to say to him, needed to say to him, *should* say to him.

They made their way through the park and back to where they started. Amanda stood by her car. She faced Thorn. "This was really nice. Thank you."

"You're welcome."

Amanda shifted from side to side. "I'd like to do this again. If *you'd* like to."

"Of course, I would."

Hearing those words from him excited her, but would he want to see her, be with her, or get close to her if he knew everything? She didn't know, and that was one of her fears.

They ended their coffee date, and she went to work, but throughout the day, she thought about all the things she didn't like people to know about her. Eventually, Thorn would find them out, and what would he think? Few men would want to deal with her neurosis. Even fewer would care to try. Women like her were called "damaged," but that word didn't even begin to describe her and what she dealt with on every given day. On the other side of the token, she hated that term. She may have been broken—her mind, her heart, her bones—but her spirit had never been broken. Nor was she damaged. She was fierce, whole, scarred but beautiful.

That evening, she completed her three consecutive trips through her house to make sure it was secured. This behavior started after she moved to Florida, after Damon. Three times each, she checked every window and door. She pushed on the front door and wrenched the deadbolts to the left, being positive they were turned as far as they could go. Then she shifted the Christmas tree box full of books to block the door, which she figured would make it difficult for Damon to shove open the door, if he managed to pick the locks and cut the two chains. If he got the door open wide enough to squeeze in, she hoped he'd trip over it.

At the windows, she made sure they were locked

and the blinds were turned up, because if they were down, he could see through the cracks. The curtains were stretched across the panes on each side, and her *Home Alone*-inspired traps were in position to alert her of an intruder. In front of one window was a sheet of bubble wrap. In front of another, she had laid out mouse traps, and at yet another, she put down a layer of cereal that would pop loudly when stepped on. Every morning, she swept the cereal into a dustpan and threw it out. Whenever she grocery shopped and bought cereal, that's what it was used for. She didn't have the money or expertise to set up lasers and other elaborate systems. In fact, she preferred her method. And sure, if Damon broke a window, she'd be able to hear the glass breaking, but what if she ever made a mistake and a window wasn't locked as she had thought? Hence the booby traps of noisy objects.

Finished, she headed for her bedroom. The second she got in, she closed and locked the door behind her. It, too, had two chains to delay Damon's entry. In her bathroom, she slid a small, wooden board in front of the window to prevent entry, but she also had a way of escape from out that window. A bar was screwed into the wall above it, and a step ladder was set up beneath it. If she ever had to flee from her bedroom, she'd lock herself in the bathroom, smash the window with the hammer on the ledge, and use the bar and stool to get out. For weeks, she had thought of every possible scenario. That's what you do if you have an abusive ex turned stalker.

Her phone chimed when she stopped at the sink to brush her teeth. She checked it, and a smile instantly manifested on her face; Thorn had texted her.

I had a great day after our coffee date.

She tapped out a reply. *So did I.*

Goodnight, Amanda.

Night.

She set down her phone, grinning from ear to ear. She picked up her toothbrush and looked up into the mirror. Her smiling face greeted her. Slowly, that smile faded. Whenever she so much as felt a hint of happiness, Damon always swooped in to demolish it.

Chapter Three

Thorn not-so-patiently waited for a week to pass after their coffee date before asking Amanda for another date. He didn't want to push her too much too soon, so he sent her a text about having lunch together at The Fighting Chance. The minutes following his text were agonizing. He paced inside the bull pen of the Orlando Police Department, gripping his phone. Everyone assumed he was waiting for contact from an informant. When his phone dinged, he came to a halt. His hands sweated as he checked the screen.

Sure. Is today too soon?

Thorn's heart skipped a beat. "Holy shit," he said aloud, causing several cops to look at him. He checked the time on his wristwatch. His lunchbreak would start in an hour. Hell no, today wasn't too soon.

He replied back, *Today is great. Do you like Thai food?*

Absolutely.

See you soon.

"Yes." Thorn let out a whoop of joy.

"Good news?" a nearby detective asked.

"The best," he confirmed.

He went to his favorite Thai restaurant. Since he didn't know what she liked, he ordered two servings each of pad thai, stir-fried rice noodles with eggs and seafood; som tum, a spicy green papaya salad; tom yam kung, a spicy shrimp soup; and kai med ma muang, stir-fried chicken with cashew nuts. With his large bag of food, he drove to The Fighting Chance. Beside the parking lot sat a cute bench beneath a cluster of palm trees. He'd seen it countless times and often spotted people having a picnic, drinking coffee, or reading a book at that bench. No one sat there now, and he thought it would be a nice place to have lunch with Amanda. Private, but not too intimate.

Carrying the bag of food, he entered The Fighting Chance. Amanda was alone behind the desk, and the space where classes took place was deserted. He didn't even see Beth or April. No doubt they had cleared out of there to give them privacy, which he appreciated.

"Hey." He stepped up to the counter. "I hope you're hungry."

"I am. I always work up a good appetite." She looked at the bag. "Although, I think you're trying to feed a small troop."

He chuckled. "I didn't know what you liked, and I got two servings each." He shrugged. "I'll have really good leftovers for a while." He glanced out the glass door. "Would you like to eat outside? There's a bench off to the side with good shade."

Amanda bit her bottom lip and gazed out the door. "Umm." She stared out there for a long moment, as if expecting to see something. Or someone.

Thorn looked, too. Did Damon know where she worked? Had he come here before? Was that why she was afraid to have lunch outside?

"Could we eat in here?" She pointed to the far side of the room where a small table was set up.

"Of course. Whatever you want."

They set out the food across the table, filling it. But something was missing. Thorn went to the front desk and came back with one of the potted orchids. "And for the finishing touch." He set the orchid in the middle of the table.

Amanda sat down across from him, and they ate silently. Several minutes went by as they tasted each dish. The silence grew between them, putting pressure on him to speak. Surely, that's what you're supposed to do during a date. Even a lunch date. Heck, he wouldn't know. He didn't date. He worked. But he wanted this to go well.

"Do you like it?" He looked up to see her face, but the orchid was in the way.

When Thorn dodged to the right to see her, she did the same, so they still couldn't see each other. He shifted to the left at the same time as she shifted to the left on her side of the table. Amanda laughed, and Thorn moved the orchid out of the way.

"That's what I get for trying to be romantic," he joked.

Amanda's smile froze. She stared at him, unblinking.

Had he said something wrong?

She swallowed. "Romantic," she said in a soft voice and lowered her gaze to the food. Her cheeks turned a gentle shade of pink.

Shit.

Thorn tried to think of a way to make this right, but before he could open his mouth, Amanda said, "It's been a long time since someone's done anything romantic for me." She peered back at him from beneath her lashes. "You're a good man, Thorn."

Now his own cheeks burned. "I try to be."

She shook her head. "You don't have to try. You are."

Silence stretched between them again. After a moment, Amanda picked up her fork and continued to eat. He did the same.

They ate without speaking, and Thorn ran over what happened a dozen times in his head. Wasn't being a good man a good thing? If that made her uncomfortable because she wasn't used to being around or being cared for by a good guy, then he was screwed. He was what he was. He wanted to show her that good men existed, that a good man loved her. His heart beat double-time at that thought. It was the first time he had allowed himself to think it, but damn it, he did love her. He'd loved her for a long time. But he feared he wouldn't be able to show her how much he loved her, would never be able to say it to her. And would never get it in return.

"Thorn."

He looked up to find Amanda studying him.

She took a deep breath before saying, "You make me laugh."

"I like the sound of your laugh," he said.

She smiled, and then she pointed at her face. "You make me smile."

"You have a beautiful smile."

At that, her smile widened. "You make me feel happy…and safe." Her smile faded, though. "That's a lot to ask of someone."

He shook his head. "You're not asking."

She took another deep breath and lowered her gaze. "But in a way, I am. When someone relies on another for their happiness and security, it puts a strain on the other person. That stress, that responsibility can be too much."

"Not for me," he cut in.

She squeezed her eyelids shut. "You say that now, but you don't know. Loved ones of abused people suffer as much but in different ways. They can resent their loved one and choose to abandon them for their own happiness and safety."

Thorn reached across the table and laid his hand over hers. "I'm not going anywhere."

Amanda's wide-eyed gaze latched onto their touching hands. He looked at them, too, and his whole body tensed. Questions exploded in his mind.

Why did I do that? Is this too much? She looks terrified. Should I remove my hand?

He pulled his hand slowly back. When his fingers no longer touched hers, he slid his hand in reverse to his side of the table. Before he moved his hand far enough away, though, Amanda stretched out her arm. The tips of her fingers touched his, as if to still them, to keep them there. He froze and didn't take his gaze off her fingers as they slipped up to his knuckles and then shifted slightly to move back down between his fingers. He moved his own fingers, so the tips of his touched hers. Gradually, their fingers came together, sliding together until they were loosely linked.

Thorn glanced at Amanda. She still looked at their hands, and her breathing had quickened. Her chest rose and fell rapidly. His own heart pounded with excitement.

"Amanda." Beth came down the hall.

Amanda jumped, yanking her hand from his.

"Yeah?" She started to rise from her chair.

"Oh, I'm sorry." Beth stopped a foot from the wall. "I didn't know the two of you were still eating. I'll get April to help me with the supplies. Take your time. You have fifteen minutes before the early arrivals come."

And Beth left them.

Amanda eased back into her chair and grasped her hands in her lap. He watched her breathe in and out, as if she were gearing herself up for something. Her gaze flicked up to his. "Can…can we talk?"

He nodded. "Yeah."

She peered around the studio and then at the door. "In your car?"

His brows lowered a fraction. "Sure."

They boxed up the leftovers, leaving half for her.

Thorn held the door open for her. At his car, he unlocked the passenger door and closed it after she sat down. In the driver's seat, he inserted the key to turn on the air conditioning. Then they sat there quietly. He didn't want to speak first, didn't want to press her about what she wanted to talk about. Instead, he waited, letting her decide when to speak and how to say whatever she needed to tell him.

She fidgeted in the passenger seat, as if struggling to get comfortable. He wondered if being so close in a confined space bothered her.

"I—" She inhaled. "I want to tell you everything." Her hands crossed defensively across her middle. He was about to tell her she didn't have to, but she was already saying, "From the beginning, Damon was destructive."

Thorn clenched his jaw. How he hated that bastard's name.

"He hit me almost daily. At first, he never marked my face. Only where I could hide the bruises. And I did. Out of shame. If I didn't answer his call, I got punished. If my text's 'tone' was rude, more punishment. If I looked at him in a way he didn't like, wham!"

Thorn balled his hands into fists.

"He didn't like me to see my family or my friends. He wanted me to go to work and come back home. If I stopped at the store and didn't tell him, he'd be waiting for me, with a beer in one hand and a belt in the other. I was his prisoner." She licked her lips and hugged herself tighter. "He installed a door handle with double-sided locks on the bedroom door. I couldn't leave unless he let me. Even when he was asleep, he'd lock the door so I couldn't get out. He'd wear the key around his neck, under his shirt. He even installed bars on the windows."

She turned her head to look out the passenger window. "People always ask 'why didn't you leave?' We all want to get away from our abusers. But I was…terrified…of him. He took away my phone, watched my bank accounts, and followed me to work every day. Eventually, he started to show up at the end of the day, to follow me back home. I didn't know how to get away."

She fell silent, and Thorn listened to her breathing. What she had told him was more than he had hoped for. What she said next, though, gutted him.

"He was sexually abusive, too. The first time we were together was my first time ever. He was rough. Too rough. I asked him to stop, but he didn't. Then he apologized. That was his thing. Abuse, apology, abuse, apology. On a loop. Day in and day out. I believed his sorrys at first, until the abuse spoke louder. Several times a week, he forced me to have sex with him."

She grimaced then, and her body flinched closer to the door, as if remembering, as if repulsed at being so close to a man. Damn, Thorn was repulsed at himself for being a man.

"One day, on my way to work, I went through a yellow light at the last second, and he raced after me through a red light, striking a car. That was my moment. I sped out of there, right for the highway and didn't stop driving until midnight. His own aggression and control helped me to finally get away. But not before the damage had been done." Her voice became thick with emotion. "I'm terrified of him to this day. My house isn't a home, but a fortress to make it impossible for him to get in. Or if he gets in, there are traps everywhere to alert me of his presence. I have hiding places and escape routes and weapons in random places. My knives are in a cabinet, not a drawer. The drawers in my kitchen are full of non-lethal items, like napkins and paper plates. I carry Mace and a Taser with me everywhere I go. There's more, too. I'm full of neuroses. If I told you how messed up he'd made me, you'd run away."

Now Thorn had to say something. "That's not true. I care about you, Amanda. More than you know." He didn't know if that was smart to tell her or not, but he had to let her know. "You could have a moat full of alligators, and I wouldn't blink an eye. You could have booby traps with swinging blades, and I wouldn't care. You could have a pit of poisonous snakes, and all I'd want to know is where it is so I don't accidentally fall in." He shifted toward her, wanting to take her hand, but he restrained himself. "I've seen your house, remember?" Last year, he had gone there to install a peephole spy camera so she'd know if Damon had come around. "Your house is what I expected it to be, and because I care about you so much, I almost suggested that moat, those alligators, and the swinging blades."

She cracked a smile then, even as a tear slipped down her cheek.

"There's nothing you could tell me that would make me run away. I'm a cop. I've seen it all. I know what abused women go through and what they have to do to feel a sense of security. I understand."

She nodded, but she didn't look at him. "What he did to me made me scared of other people, especially men. It took me a long time to be okay with being touched again." She rubbed her hands together. "Beth helped me." She glanced at him. "*You* helped me."

He thought she was finished when she didn't speak for a couple of minutes, but then she said, "He broke my arm."

Startled by that, Thorn angled his neck to her.

"He snapped a few of my ribs…busted my eardrum…dragged me by my hair…kicked me in the stomach…" She lifted her hands. They shook as she pulled down the zipper to the pink workout vest, revealing a matching sports bra underneath and a pale pink scar. It was about four inches long. "He s-stabbed me."

Thorn looked away and gripped the steering wheel with his right hand.

"He lacerated my liver. I lost a lot of

blood…almost died."

Thorn's grip tightened. The leather groaned. He inhaled and exhaled sharply. His rage from what that asshole did to her was fierce. If he could get his hands on Damon at this moment, he'd kill him. But then a warm, soft hand enclosed around his. He blinked away his anger to see Amanda's hand resting over his on the steering wheel. One by one, she pried his fingers from the leather, forcing him to relax his hand. Then she brought it to her lap, where she cradled it in her hands. He stared at her hands holding his. This time, he didn't even try to lace their fingers together, but let her calm fill him through the form of touch she could handle. Eventually, he turned his head to look through the windshield, as she was doing. And, so, they sat there together in his car, just like that.

After a while, a couple students for the next lesson arrived, and yet, Amanda didn't move to leave. He wondered if she would, but he also didn't want this moment to end.

She rotated in the seat toward him. Before he could look at her, one of her hands came around and cradled the side of his face, and she pressed her lips to his cheek. She held it there for several heartbeats. Then she laid her forehead against his temple.

The desire to kiss her overwhelmed him, but he dared not move. She inched back to kiss his cheek again. In the next instant, she opened the car door and hurried into the studio.

Chapter Four

Amanda slammed into the door of the studio, shoving it open, stumbling inside. Her heart raced. She couldn't breathe. A cold sweat broke out on her forehead, palms, and back. Her mouth went dry. Why couldn't she swallow? Why the hell couldn't she see anything? Her vision was black. She walked blindly forward, needing to escape.

"Amanda, what's wrong?" Beth's voice came to her. A second later, hands took her arms. She flinched.

"What's wrong?" Beth demanded.

She blinked, and Beth came into view.

"What happened?" Beth peered over her shoulder. "Did he do something?"

"N-no. I did. I held his h-hand. I kissed his ch-cheek."

"But you've danced with him and kissed him before."

Amanda shook her head as tears formed. This was different. "I told him e-every-th-thing." She put a hand to her chest. "W-why can't I b-breathe?"

"You're having a panic attack. Come on." Beth hurried her to the office where she closed the door for privacy and ushered Amanda to the love seat. Amanda sat down as Beth turned the fan on full blast and directed it toward her. After switching on the CD player, Beth came over with a paper cup of water.

"Here. Take a sip."

Her hand wobbled when she brought the cup to her lips. She struggled to catch a sip and then to swallow it.

Beth took the seat next to her and placed a hand on her knee. "Now tell me three things you see."

Amanda focused on her surroundings, picking out the things she could see. "Your desk."

She looked to Beth. "You." And then her gaze dropped to the floor. "My shoes."

"That's good. Tell me three things you hear."

Amanda strained to hear something other than the pounding of her heart. "Music." A soothing melody came from the CD player.

"Voices." More and more students were arriving. "And my voice."

"You're doing perfect. What are three things you smell?"

Amanda inhaled deeply through her nose. "Sweat." She let out her breath and took another deep breath. "Disinfectant spray and your perfume."

"Now three things you feel."

Amanda reconnected to the rest of her body. First, she felt a reassuring pressure and warmth on her knee. "Your hand." Then the feeling in her own hands returned. "The cool water in the cup." She took another centering breath. "My heart." Which continued to pound hard but not as fast.

"And one thing you taste."

She unstuck her tongue from the roof of her mouth, felt the saliva pooling at the bottom of her mouth, and swallowed. "Thai food. I probably have bad breath."

Beth let out a small laugh at that, and Amanda managed a tiny smile in return. Beth rubbed her leg.

"Can you tell me what happened?"

Amanda took a sip of water before answering. "I revealed everything to him. I even showed him my scar. You could imagine what that did to him."

Beth nodded.

"I didn't want him to be angry, so I held his hand. But his reaction…I didn't know someone could feel that for me. So, I kissed his cheek. Immediately after that, everything came crashing down. The things I feel for him are too strong. I can't handle it."

"Yes, you can," Beth assured her. "You feel those things because you *can* handle them."

She stared at Beth, and a tear broke loose. "I'm scared."

"I know you are." Beth wrapped her arms around Amanda, who held onto her friend as if she were a life preserver, and Beth didn't let go until Amanda did. "Take your time. Stay in here for as long as you need."

"Thanks."

While Beth and April taught the class, Amanda lay down on the love seat, with her legs curled, and closed her eyes. She tried to clear her mind, but she kept thinking about the feel of Thorn's hand in hers, how she had wanted to kiss his lips, not just his cheek, and the things he said to her. He truly was a good man. He was built that way. No, born that way. He didn't have an abusive bone in his body. He could love her, if she allowed him.

Beth knocked on the door. "Hey, how are you feeling?"

Amanda sat up, confused. "Is the class over?"

"Yeah." Beth observed her a moment. "Why don't you go home? You can rest, take a nice bath, eat some chocolate."

Amanda smiled. "Are you sure?"

"About the chocolate? Absolutely." She squeezed Amanda's shoulder. "I'm sure. You had a turning point today. An important one. You need time to rejuvenate."

Amanda took Beth's words to heart. As soon as she got home, she took a hot bath, had a glass of wine, and ate a chocolate bar. Although Beth hadn't mentioned wine, Amanda figured she'd approve anyway. That night, before bed, Thorn sent her a text consisting of five words.

I'm glad you told me.

She wasn't sure if she was glad she told him, though, so she didn't respond.

In the morning, he sent this text. *Are you okay*?

Was she? She didn't know, so she still didn't reply.

What she did know was she wasn't ready for anything today. She called Beth at home. "Hi, umm, I need to call out sick."

"Are you okay?" Beth asked the same question Thorn had wanted to know.

"I don't feel good today."

"Okay. I hope you feel better. Take care."

"Bye." Amanda hung up, feeling cowardly.

She stayed inside her house, wrapped in a blanket. Occasionally, she paced, but mostly she curled up on her bed. After lunchtime, another text from Thorn came in.

I stopped in at The Fighting Chance. You weren't there. Please tell me you're okay.

"I can't do that," she said to her phone. "Because I'm not sure if I'm okay. And if I tell you I'm not okay, you're going to want to see me, and I can't. I can't do that, either. I can't handle seeing you or being around you right now. And it's not because of you. It's because of me." She could've told him all that, but she was afraid to admit those things. Despite her words that it wasn't because of him, he'd think it was, and she didn't want that.

He didn't text her again until the next morning. *Amanda, please. I'm a cop. When no one sees you or hears from you, I think the worst. Text me back a single word to let me know you're safe.*

Amanda closed her eyes.

Inhale, exhale.

Inhale, exhale.

Inhale, exhale.

She opened her eyes.

The text remained, and on the other side of it, Thorn waited.

She tapped her finger to the spot where she could type out a response. The keyboard popped up. Her finger hovered over it. She could say "okay." That would be short and to the point. Or she could say "hi," which would be lighter. Neither option she liked very much, so she touched a single button and sent him a period.

Right away, the three dots appeared, telling her he was typing.

Thank you.

And with those two words, he conveyed his relief. That relief broke her. She threw her phone across the room, collapsed into a ball on the floor, and cried.

Chapter Five

The day after Amanda sent the period text message, Thorn went to Beth and Donovan's house. The twins sat in side by side highchairs. Bits of scrambled eggs were scattered across their trays. Ryan reached over to his sister and smeared tiny pieces of eggs in her dark hair. Thorn pressed his lips together.

Your secret is safe with me, lil man.

"Do you want coffee?" Beth asked him.

"Yeah."

"Eggs?"

He looked at the remains of the eggs on the twins' highchairs. "I'll pass."

Beth passed him a cup of black coffee, and they sat down at the table occupied by Donovan. Thorn watched the four of them interact, envying what they had, which surprised him. He wanted Amanda, but he didn't know if he wanted kids and the whole shebang.

"What's on your mind?" Beth asked him.

He stared into his coffee.

"You might as well tell her. She'll pry it out of you sooner or later," Donovan said.

Thorn sighed. "I keep thinking I did something wrong with Amanda."

"You didn't."

He met Beth's eye. "Did she tell you?"

Beth nodded. "It's not anything you did. It's what

she did. Telling you all that was huge for her. She probably told you things she hasn't even told me."

"I feel as though she's running away from me now, and I'm never going to get her back."

Beth and Donovan exchanged glances.

"What is it?" he asked.

Donovan nodded at Beth.

She looked back to Thorn. "When Amanda came inside, she was having a panic attack."

"What?" That realization horrified him.

Beth put her hand on his arm. "Remember, it wasn't because of you."

"But in a way it was." And that sliced him to shreds. "Am I really good for her if I cause her panic attacks?"

"Yes." Beth looked him right in the eye and repeated, "Yes. You are good for her, and she's good for you. Give her some time."

He gazed off into space. All he'd been doing was giving her time. He wasn't sure how much more he had left to give. At the same time, if she needed it, he wouldn't deny her that. How could he?

He couldn't.

Time. Such a little word. Fleeting in reality, but grand in the scope of things.

He didn't send Amanda another text message, even while hoping she'd send him one. The next day, when he was scheduled to help out with the classes for young kids at The Fighting Chance, he told Beth he couldn't make it. He loved taking part in those classes, but he didn't know what to do around Amanda if she didn't want to be near him. That's why he backed out of the Sunday classes, too.

Come Monday, he couldn't keep cancelling, couldn't keep putting off the inevitable. He had a beginner's class he needed to speak to, and he didn't want to cut from that class, too. Him not talking to those students today could result in dire consequences. One of those students may need his advice as soon as tonight. So, he pulled on his big boy pants and went to The Fighting Chance for the morning beginner's class. When he stepped inside, Amanda's back was to him as she set out the equipment, and he walked right past her to Beth's office. Even as he did it, he hated himself for being chicken shit. He couldn't avoid her forever.

When all the students arrived, he stood at the front of the room beside Beth. Amanda joined them, forced to stand next to him. Trying not to focus on her presence, he went through his talk, giving the advice that only a cop could provide. Afterward, he usually assisted with showing them techniques for getting out of the most common holds perpetrators used. Today, he was supposed to walk them through escaping the choke hold. He thought Beth would be his partner for this, but she shook her head.

"I thought Amanda could assist you today."

He glared at her, not believing she'd do this. Then again, it was her style.

Cursing inside, he faced Amanda. "The first one we're going to show is the front choke hold." He hated what he was going to say next. "Most commonly used by intimate partners." He stared into Amanda's eyes, searching for any sign of her not wanting to proceed.

She nodded for him to continue.

Clenching his jaw, he put his hands on either side of her neck, but he didn't apply any pressure. "To get out of this hold, you'd want to raise your right arm, turn your body, and then chop down on your attacker's arm. This will force your attacker to release his hold."

Amanda demonstrated the steps slowly and even mimicked fleeing. When she came back, he replaced his hands, and they went through the motions again, but faster.

"Another method is to bend forward and spin around so you twist out of the hold."

They went through that one a couple of times.

"If an attacker does the same hold from the back, same thing as the first technique but in reverse." Amanda turned her back to him, and he put his hands around her again. "Arm up," he said, "and then spin around. Your arm will come across the attacker's arms, breaking his hold."

As before, they practiced it once, and then they did it at full speed.

Once they completed those, he looked to Beth, wanting to be cut some slack, but she wasn't going to let him off the hook. "There's one more they're going to demonstrate," she said to the class. "And then we'll all be able to practice."

Amanda knew what was coming; she got down on the mat and lay flat. Thorn inhaled sharply before kneeling over her. Shaking his head, he put his hands into position. While looking into her eyes, he addressed the students. "Now you'll want to bend your left knee and put your left foot on the other side of the attacker's shin, which is against the floor." Amanda did as he said. "From there, you bend your right knee and put the bottom of your foot flat on the floor, too. Once you do that, pivot with your hip." Amanda did that until she was on top. She quickly hopped to her feet, leaving him lying there. "As you can see, you switch your position with the attacker's. He then lets go of you, and you are now free to escape."

He got to his feet, relieved that was finally over. For the rest of the lesson, the students practiced each method, and the three of them assisted. By the end of it, Thorn wanted to make a run for it himself, but he stayed put while the students filed out. Amanda went behind the receptionist's desk to jot down notes from the class.

He faced Beth and said under his breath, "Don't ever do that to me again."

She grimaced. "Sorry. It was tough love. For the both of you."

"Yeah, yeah, yeah. I love you, too."

He headed for the door. Except, no matter how much he wanted to walk out, pretend Amanda wasn't there, he couldn't. Already regretting it, he paused at the desk and drummed the counter with his finger nervously. "That period," he said, "was beautiful." He rapped his finger a couple more times before turning to leave.

"Wait."

Amanda rushed around the desk, surprising him. That desk had always been a safety barrier between them. At times, he had been grateful for it. Other times, he had wanted to smash it with a sledgehammer. Once she was on his side, Amanda stopped in front of him. When she sprang forward and threw her arms around him, she couldn't have surprised him more.

"I'm sorry," she said. "I was working through something."

Before he could put his arms around her in return, she stepped back. "I'm better, though." Her gaze dropped, and she picked at her nail. A second later, she put her arms behind her back and lifted her chin so her gaze met his. "Would you like to go to dinner with me?"

Thorn smiled. "I thought you'd never ask."

Chapter Six

"You asked him out?" April's jaw dropped.

Amanda nodded. "I did."

"I'm proud of you," Beth said.

"I'm proud of me, too."

"When is the dinner?" April wanted to know.

"Friday."

April clapped her hands. "And please tell me I wasn't the only one who saw the tension during the demonstration. It was kinda hot." She fanned herself with her hand. "I mean, Thorn is sexy, but that was H.O.T."

"It was hot because it was Thorn," Beth said, causing Amanda and April to stare at her with raised brows.

"Isn't he like your brother?" April asked.

"From another mother, yeah." Beth rolled her eyes. "I mean because he's gentle and cautious."

April nodded. "Hot." She waggled a brow at Amanda. "Did you feel it?"

"I did."

"Did it scare you?" Beth said.

"A little, but it…excited me more."

"Yeah, it did," April said and nudged Amanda with her elbow.

That night, Amanda thought about Thorn. It wasn't as though she hadn't thought about being intimate with him before, because she had. Many times. Most of the time, she imagined it to be sweet and passionate. Occasionally, though, Thorn would morph into Damon, and that sweetness would be a lie disguised as brutality. She'd wake up screaming. For the rest of the night, she'd repeat, "Thorn wouldn't do that. Thorn wouldn't do that. Thorn wouldn't do that."

Damon had planted seeds of fear in her, and they grew bigger as she got closer to Thorn. One day, she wanted to take a machete to them, a chainsaw, a damn sickle. She'd massacre what he did. Every hurt. Every memory. Every fear and tear. Nothing would be left, and in the place where Damon had ruined her, Thorn would be there, healing her. He already was there, but Damon's vines were surrounding him, like an evil wall of thorns.

Thorns.

Amanda woke up the next morning full of curiosity. She only ever knew Thorn as Thorn. That's what everyone called him. He was Detective Thorn, but that was his last name. *Wasn't it*? She wasn't sure, but cops usually went by their last names, like teachers, doctors, and other professionals. So…what was Thorn's first name?

She went to work, pondering that. While she assisted Beth with setting out the equipment, she took the opportunity. "Beth?"

"Yeah?"

She set a helmet on the mat. "What's Thorn's first name?"

Beth stood up straight and directed a wide smile at Amanda.

"What?"

Beth's smile grew.

"Do you know it?"

"Of course, I do," Beth said.

"What is it?" She wanted to know so badly her body jittered with excitement.

"You'll have to ask him yourself during your date on Friday."

Amanda gaped at her. "But that's three days away."

"Uh-huh. It is." Beth smiled. "If you can't wait that long, you can ask him sooner, but I'm not going to tell you."

"Is it an embarrassing name?" Maybe that was why he didn't use it.

"I'm not going to say."

Amanda put a hand on her hip. "Seriously?"

Beth straightened even more, unwavering. "Seriously."

Amanda let out a huff. "Fine. I'll ask him."

"Good."

That smile Beth wore—what did it mean? Was this another one of Beth's ways to help the two of them get closer? Like the demonstration yesterday?

The whole day, she tried to guess his name.

David Thorn.

Michael Thorn.

Ethan Thorn.

Nothing she came up with fit him, though. They were all good names, but they weren't Thorn. She picked up one of his business cards from the counter, but as she already knew, it didn't have his first name on it. Curiosity had her going to the computer and eyeing the search bar. She stopped herself from typing in

"Detective Thorn/Orlando Police Department," though. If she did, she might find an article or the department's employee list. Suddenly, she didn't want to spoil the secret by looking him up on the Internet.

On Wednesday, she studied him from head to toe when he stopped in to speak to students one on one. A few of them had gone through situations recently and wanted his advice, and he agreed to listen to anyone who wanted to talk to him. He didn't have a medical ID or dog tags. On his left wrist, he wore a silver watch, and a silver band occupied his ring finger.

Silver Thorn?

She shook her head. While "Silver Thorn" was cool, she wasn't sure someone would name a child "Silver." Then again, it was possible.

She tilted her head while looking at him. *Silver*. It sounded too exotic for him.

Her gaze went back to the ring he wore. More questions emerged.

When he left, she immediately went to Beth. "You know the ring Thorn wears?"

"On his ring finger?" Beth asked as she wiped the inside of a helmet with an antibacterial wipe.

"Yeah." Amanda pulled a wipe from the container and got to work on another helmet. "Was he married?" She squinted at Beth, checking for any hint of a facial change. "Did she die?"

Beth's neck snapped up. "No. No, it's nothing like that. He's never been married."

Amanda's shoulders lowered. "Okay, but…why does he wear it?"

"You know what I'm going to say."

A sigh left Amanda's lips. "Ask him."

"Yup."

Now she had two questions to ask him. Two questions that might be personal. Perhaps it was time for her to learn personal information about him. After all, she'd had the courage to share her story, her pain, with him. Her interest meant she was ready to know more about him, and that was a big step forward. She couldn't wait to ask him. In the past, she would've rolled them into a tiny ball and buried them down. She would've nailed a Restricted sign over its hiding place. No more did she want to deny herself what she wanted.

Come Thursday, she was anxious and nervous and looking forward to their date. She didn't know where Thorn would want to meet her or what she'd wear, but right now, that didn't matter. What mattered was the fact she wanted to go. That she wanted to spend time with him. Be near him. Feel him.

Be.

With him.

She had never thought she'd get to this point. Not when she was trapped in Damon's grasp. Not when she was running for her life. Not when she was too scared to leave her home.

Thorn had healed her. Just by being there. The first time he had spoken to the advanced class she was a member of, hiding in the back row, he had started to cure her. His business card had been a dose of medicine that gave her strength. She hadn't known him personally then, but she had someone in her corner, someone she could call in a time of need. She realized from his first talk that Thorn was a fighter for people like her. For weeks, she spoke to him privately in her thoughts. He'd listen. He'd say the right thing. He was a beacon.

Then when Beth introduced them, a veil had been lifted. Amanda felt as though she already knew him, because she knew the version of him who lived inside her mind. And he was as she had imagined him to be—caring, strong, dependable. But more, too. Talking to him in real life was daunting, but if she could do it in her head, she could make the words come out of her mouth. It took a lot of courage, and that's what he had given her. Later, she'd imagined touching him. Kissing him. Both were infinitely better in reality.

She found herself daydreaming a lot throughout the day. The last class left, and the three of them stood behind the front desk chatting while completing paperwork, munching on snacks, and waiting for the last ten minutes of their workday to go by so they could flip the open sign and begin cleaning up.

Amanda looked up from the current list of up-to-date payments for classes. A movement outside the glass storefront caught her eye. She tilted her head to see a man coming up the sidewalk from the side where the picnic bench sat. Through the vertical blinds, she glimpsed a square face—a short, rugged beard and long, dark hair pulled into a man bun. Her breath fled from her lungs. Her body went from icy cold to flaming hot in the span of a millisecond. She dropped to the floor and slid under the counter, beneath the ledge where they put their purses and cell phones.

"What—" Beth peeked at the windows. Then she snapped her fingers at April and pointed at the stools.

April jumped into action. She pushed the stools in so they blocked Amanda. The bell attached to the door jingled as April removed the jacket she wore and draped it across the stools, creating a curtain to shield Amanda.

From a crack, Amanda watched Beth move to stand in front of the twins, who were in their walkers playing peacefully. “I’m sorry, but we’re going to be closing.”

“I don’t give a shit. I’m here for Amanda.”

The sound of Damon’s voice had her heart beating even harder. That voice had haunted her nightmares, had come back to life in her memories.

Beth cocked her head to the side. “Who? There’s no one by that name here.”

“Don’t bullshit me. I know she works here.”

His voice was closer now.

“I don’t know who you’re talking about.”

Through the crack, Damon came into view. He wore dark jeans, combat boots, a tight black shirt, and leather bands on his arm. Even his sleeve tattoo was visible.

She swallowed. Those arms had restrained her when she’d tried to run away from his attacks. Those hands had punched her. Those same boots had kicked her.

“Bitch, you don’t know who you’re messing with.”

“If you don’t leave now, I’m going to call the police.”

“Fuck the police. I’m not leaving without Amanda.”

He took a couple of strides toward the hall, but Beth cut him off.

“Even if I knew who you were looking for, do you really think I’d let her leave with you?”

He took a threatening step toward her. “You

wouldn't have a choice," he snarled. "Now, get out of my fucking way." He took another step, and Amanda braced for the hit she expected him to give Beth. "Move!"

His shouts made Ryan break out into tears. He cried so hard his lips quivered. His outburst prompted Reagan to sob, too. The twins' wails were deafening.

Damon stomped toward them. "Shut them up!"

Beth jumped in front of the twins, putting her arms out to protect them. "If you come near my kids, I will rip you to shreds," she growled.

April sprang forward. She grabbed Ryan's walker and pulled it all the way behind the counter. She did the same with Reagan, putting them side by side. Then she planted herself in front of them. Through the crack, past April's leg, Amanda watched Beth going toe to toe with Damon. His hands were in fists at his sides. He didn't like it when women stood up to him. It only made him angrier.

"I'm not here for you or your brats, lady. I'm here for Amanda."

"Once again. She's. Not. Here."

Damon nodded, not believing her. "Fine. Tell her I'll be back."

He turned.

"If you come back here, I'll call the cops."

His voice came from behind Amanda, making her flinch. "Do it."

The bell rattled, and the door slammed shut.

Beth disappeared from her line of vision and so did April.

The lock on the door clunked, and the blinds clattered as they shut.

"Holy shit," April whispered. "I thought he was going to deck you."

"Ssh," Beth said.

The farthest stool moved out of the way, taking with it April's jacket. Beth squatted down in the space. "It's okay. You can come out." She reached for Amanda and took her hands.

Amanda crawled out. As soon as she stood up, she peered over her shoulder at the storefront, but the windows were covered. Instantly, her body broke into uncontrollable jitters. Her chest tightened as if a metal band had vised around it, like a torture device and Damon was on the other end of it, twisting the bolts to make it tighter and tighter. She gasped for breath. Tears erupted from her eyes, and the next thing she knew, she was crying hysterically.

"April, stay with the twins." Beth escorted Amanda to the office.

Once again, she sat on the love seat. Her head spun, and her stomach quivered. "I feel sick," she said.

Beth grabbed the trashcan and put it at her feet.

"Why do I feel sick?"

"You're in shock." Beth spread a blanket over her shoulders. Next to her, she wrapped a supportive arm around Amanda and stroked her arms.

Amanda wanted to run, but she felt as though she was going to vomit. And the tears wouldn't stop. She gripped the trashcan, hyperventilating. Beside her, Beth offered her words of encouragement that fell on deaf ears. She didn't know how long she spewed tears and struggled to breathe, but her eyes and cheeks dried and her breathing evened out. Dazed, she stared into the trashcan at the crumpled pieces of paper and a snack-sized potato chip bag. The colors swam in her vision, blending together. She lifted her head, stared at the wall. The gray-ish blue paint consumed her, pulled her in like a wormhole.

"Amanda?"

The trashcan disappeared from her loose grip.

"Amanda?"

A second later, Beth shouted for April, but she sounded far away, at the end of a mile-long tunnel.

"What's wrong with her?" April's voice echoed softly, as if it bounced along the walls of Amanda's head, which was uselessly hollow.

"This is a symptom of emotional shock. You can feel out of your body and disconnected."

"What do we do?"

"Call Thorn."

Beth continued to talk to Amanda, but her voice became discombobulated. Amanda couldn't understand a thing she said. Words weren't real anymore.

What *was* real?

Damon.

Chapter Seven

“The Fighting Chance” came up on Thorn’s cell phone screen. Beth usually called him on her cell, even while at work. He answered it, “This is Detective Thorn.”

“Thorn, thank God.”

“April?”

“You need to get here right now. It’s Amanda.”

He shoved to his feet, even as his heart sank. “What happened?”

“Damon was here.”

Those three words had him grabbing his keys and marching to the door. “Did he touch her?”

“No. He didn’t even see her, but…she needs you.”

“I’m on my way.”

He drove with sirens on, because if a loved one in despair wasn’t an emergency, he didn’t know what was. He swerved into the parking lot and didn’t stop fast enough when he shot into an empty space, so the bottom of his bumper scraped against the concrete. After shoving the stick shift into place and ripping the keys from the ignition, he jumped out of the car and onto the sidewalk. April waited for him inside the studio and unlocked the door to let him in.

“Where is she?”

“In Beth’s office.”

He made his way there with long strides. When he

turned into the doorway, he found Beth and Amanda sitting side by side on the love seat. A blanket was draped over Amanda's shoulders. Beth turned to him, but Amanda didn't. She continued to stare straight ahead.

"Hey," he said softly.

Still, Amanda acted as though he wasn't there.

Beth shook her head. "She's in shock. She's not talking or moving. She's barely blinking."

His heart fractured. *God, that bastard could hurt her without even laying a hand on her*. For that, he wanted to beat the man black and blue.

"I'll talk to her," he said.

Beth got up. She squeezed his arm as she left.

The door clicked behind him.

He moved around the love seat and knelt in front of Amanda. Her gaze stayed a few inches above his head. "Amanda." She didn't look at him. "It's Thorn. I'm here." He searched her face for any sign of recognition, but it was eerily blank. Her eyes were like slates wiped clean. "You're safe. Remember, I told you I'm never going to leave. I keep my word." Still, she remained immobile. He lifted his hand and laid it against her cheek. "Do you feel that?" He brought his other hand to her cheek, too, and cupped her face. "I'm here. You just have to look at me, and then you'll see I'm right here."

Her eyelids lowered slowly, but when they opened again, her gaze was still trained above him. "Amanda, please. You're stronger than him. You may not believe it, but you are. You can't be weak and have survived what you have." He rubbed the side of his thumb against her velvety skin. "I'm not going to let him hurt you again. Not on my life."

Her gaze shifted down to his face.

Relief swept through him. "There you are."

She blinked. Her brows lowered in a frown, and she blinked again. Now, she looked at him in surprise. "Thorn?" Her voice was small.

"I'm here," he repeated.

Amanda let out a breath, as if she had been holding it. Then she launched forward and coiled her arms around his neck. He slipped his arms around her, hugging her with every ounce of worry that had dominated him a moment ago. Not wanting to break their embrace, he eased off his knees and shifted onto the cushion beside her. She curled her legs beneath her and leaned into his body. He held her for a long time in the sound of silence.

"I thought…" Her voice was so soft Thorn wondered if he'd actually heard it. "I thought he wouldn't leave. He didn't want to, not without me, but Beth stood firm."

She would.

"I thought he was going to hit her. And then he went after the twins."

Thorn stiffened. That piece-of-shit went after his god kids?

"Beth blocked him, and April pulled the twins behind the counter where I was cowering. I couldn't do anything. He could've hurt them all, and I might've stayed there like a coward."

"No." He caressed her back. "Don't think about that. Nothing happened. Everyone is safe. You're safe."

She fell quiet and stayed wrapped up in his arms. He wanted to always hold her, but it was after closing hours. Beth needed to lock down the studio for the night. No doubt they all wanted to get home after the scare they'd had.

"We should go."

She nodded against his shoulder.

With a supportive arm around her shoulders, he led her out of the office. At the counter, April stood with Beth and Donovan, who must've arrived shortly after he did. Donovan had an arm around Beth's waist, and his other arm held Reagan. Beth balanced Ryan on her hip. The three of them faced Thorn and Amanda as they made their way across the studio floor. Amanda shivered under the weight of their stares.

"Are you okay?" Beth asked.

He peeked at Amanda to see her not looking at Beth but at Donovan. Her eyes were wide, petrified. Beads of sweat glistened on her forehead. She shivered again.

"I'm so sorry," she said.

Donovan frowned.

A moment later, Thorn realized what she meant. Amanda was afraid of what Donovan would do to her because of what Damon had almost done to his family…and also because of what Damon had done to her in the past. A part of her believed all men were like Damon. Even though she'd known Donovan for years, abuse had ingrained too many habits in her that she wouldn't be able to erase so easily.

Donovan must've come to the same conclusion, because he shook his head. "No, Amanda, it's not your fault."

"But it is," she whispered.

Those words, from her lips, reminded Thorn of what he'd said to Beth and Donovan, when he thought her panic attack had been because of him…because it had been. In a way, at least.

"I'll drive you home," he offered.

She shook her head. "I need my car. I can do it."

Despite her words, he worried she wouldn't be able to drive safely, but he also couldn't force her to accept a ride. "I'll make sure you get there safely then and follow you home."

"That sounds like a good idea," Beth said.

Thorn kept a watchful eye on Amanda's car, making sure it didn't swerve. From experience, he knew stress could greatly impair someone's driving, but Amanda drove steadily the whole way to her house. She must've driven, anxious and fearful, hundreds of times while Damon stalked her, followed her everywhere she went.

At her house, he pulled his car onto the grass past her mailbox to keep her car clear. Then he jogged up the driveway to Amanda. "Stay in your car with the doors locked a minute. I'm going to check your property."

Amanda's face paled. "Okay."

He waited until she got back into the driver's seat and he'd heard the doors lock before making his way around the house. A few steps beyond the corner, he glanced over his shoulder to see if Amanda could see him. When the windshield of her car was out of view, he pulled his firearm from his holster. Cradling the gun, pointing it at the ground, he searched the backyard and every place Damon could be hiding. Nothing. Pausing on the other side of the house, behind the wall, he tucked his firearm back into its holster. He walked back to her car and rapped on her window. She pushed the button to roll it down.

"Can you slip your house key from your keychain? I want to check inside."

"Keys," she corrected as she worked the loop free.

She showed him the order for which keys to use for which locks.

He unlocked them and shut the door at his back. One by one, he checked each room. Amanda had made it hard for an intruder to hide or lurk in her house, so the walk-through went quickly. When he finished, he stepped out on the front stoop and waved for her to come inside.

With her purse on her shoulder, she hustled up the walk to him. "Thanks for doing this."

"You're welcome."

"Um." She gazed down at her sneakers. "Would you like to come in? I have beer."

"I'm actually on the clock."

"Oh, right."

Her disappointment stabbed him like a screwdriver to his liver. "My shift ends at eight. I'll check in on you then."

She nodded. "I'd like that."

He wanted to kiss her on the cheek, but he didn't know how she'd react after the trauma she experienced earlier. So, he jiggled his keys. "Call me if you need me. For anything."

"I will."

"I'll stay here until I hear the second chain go on."

She smiled. "Thank you."

He did as he said he would and didn't budge from his spot until he heard each bolt click into place and both chains clatter and slide through their tracks.

"Bye, Thorn." Amanda's voice came muffled through the door.

"Bye, Amanda."

Back at work, he kept peeking at the time. He clocked out promptly at eight o'clock. Moments later, he knocked on Amanda's door.

She opened it, wearing pajamas and a surprised expression. "Thorn! I thought you were going to call to check in."

"Yeah, that would've made more sense. I'm sorry. I should've called."

"No, that's okay. I still have that beer."

Chapter Eight

The two of them sat across from each other at Amanda's kitchen table. She twirled a bottle of beer around and around in her hands. She wanted to tell Thorn so much, but she couldn't get the words past her lips. For several minutes, she debated over whether or not to ask him the two questions she'd been dying to know the answers to, but what if they didn't have anything to discuss during their date tomorrow?

She looked at Thorn. *Oh, God, does he look bored*?

"I'm sorry I'm so awkward."

Thorn looked up. His brows lowered. "What do you mean?"

"I've been trying to figure out what to say." She shrugged. "I'm awkward."

"Just being here is enough for me."

Her cheeks heated as if burned. But in a good way. A very good way.

"I mean it. I could sit with you for hours, neither of us saying a word, and I'd be happy."

She gazed at him, wondering why she ever had to live through Damon's torment if there was a man like Thorn in the world. Would she have ever met Thorn without Damon, though? That thought chilled her. No way would she thank Damon for this. No, she'd thank herself. Because she was the one who got out, who escaped, who made her way to Florida with no possessions, no clue as to what would happen next. If she had known this moment was waiting for her, she would've found some way to leave sooner. A lot sooner.

"Thank you for being patient with me," she whispered. "It can't be easy."

"It's been worth it."

She stared at him. The urge to get up and kiss him played a tug of war with her body, with the scared part of herself saying to stay seated. *Damn it. I have to get the guts to do this. I want to. I want to so badly.* She tightened her hands around the bottle. *So do it*!

She didn't move.

Her thoughts made chicken sounds at her.

"I…I like being near you. I think about the Christmas party a lot." She glanced at him, and then away. "I know you want more." Out of the corner of her eye, he fidgeted on the stool. "And I want more." That claim had him stilling. "I'm just not brave."

"That's a lie." His voice was soft. "You're one of the bravest people I know."

What she said next, she said slowly. "Sometimes I think about how…what I'm doing to you isn't fair."

"You're not doing anything to me."

"Really?" She looked him in the eye then. "One step forward. Ten steps back."

He broke eye contact with her.

As I expected. She hated knowing she'd been putting him through that. Then again, she'd been putting herself through the same torment.

"I don't want it to be like that anymore. I want to go forward from now on. With you." When he met her eyes again, she gazed into them steadily. "Forward.

With you."

"I'll go wherever you want to go."

Her lips lifted. If she had to take a step back, he'd follow. But she didn't want to go backward anymore. She'd done enough of that, all while Damon had been gone—more or less, because he was always present in her mind. In her body. It didn't matter if he was there physically or not; he still had the same effect. Except, she didn't want him to have that power anymore. Even with him there now, making his presence loud and clear, she was tired of letting him dominate her everything.

This. This she would not let him ruin.

Thorn checked his watch. "I'm sorry to say this, but I should be getting home. I have an early morning."

She got to her feet. "Um."

He paused with his keys in his hand.

"I was actually wondering…if you could…you don't have to but…could you…stay?" She swallowed. When he didn't speak, she added, "Tonight."

He blinked, and she realized what he might be thinking. She rocked forward on the balls of her feet. "On the couch." Her heart raced. "I…I don't want to be alone tonight after…" Her voice faded. She took a deep breath. "Nights are hard," she added quickly, diverting her gaze.

"I'll stay." He had said it so softly she thought she might've heard him wrong.

"What?"

"I said I'll stay."

She nodded. "Thank you."

From a closet, she found him an extra pillow and blanket. She brought them to him. "I appreciate this more than I can say."

"You don't have to say. I know."

There it was. Thorn got her, without her even having to voice a word.

"Goodnight," she said.

"See you in the morning."

She turned, feeling her stomach flutter at the idea of waking up to Thorn in her house.

That flutter wasn't panic or anxiety, though. It was thrill. She took a step before turning back and closing the distance between them. Raising her hands, she laid her palms against his chest. Then she moved her hands to either side of his neck. Her gaze settled on his mouth. She inched closer until their foreheads touched and their noses brushed. So close, she stopped moving.

His warm breath heated her lips, invigorating her. She pressed her lips to his. The memory of how his lips had felt at Beth and Donovan's Christmas party rushed back to her. Before then, the last person who had touched her lips with his was Damon. His kisses had been branding, bruising, punishing. Thorn's kisses, however, were gentle, caring, passionate. She'd forgotten how a kiss should feel.

Thorn's hands cupped her hips, and she flinched.

"I'm sorry." He lifted his hands.

"No. Put them back. I'm okay."

He took her hips again. Carefully.

She closed her eyes to imprint how they felt in her memory and nodded. "Your hands will never hurt me. I know that. My body doesn't, but it will. Eventually." She brought her lips back to his. What she loved about Thorn was he didn't try to change the kiss, deepen it, push her past her comfort zone. Their lips locked and nothing more. Yet, for her, it was everything *and* more.

"Night," she whispered, with their lips touching.

After a moment, she eased away from his comforting body heat and walked to her bedroom. She didn't look over her shoulder the entire way. In her room, though, when she'd normally shut and lock her door, she paused with the edge of the door touching the jamb. For the first time since she moved into that house, she didn't want to bar the door from anyone on the other side of it, because Thorn was on the other side.

She kept the door cracked open.

Hours later, she crept out of her room. Her footsteps were quiet as she approached the couch where Thorn slept. She gazed down at him. His arms were crossed over his chest. The blanket she had given him came up to his hips. He still wore his holstered weapon. On high alert, even while in sleep. It couldn't be comfortable. Unless he wasn't asleep.

Her eyes widened. If his eyelids flipped open and he caught her spying on him in the middle of the night, she'd forever be humiliated. She tiptoed back to her bedroom and slunk into bed. Sleeping with him nearby kept her awake for a long time.

Before she knew it, though, the sound of Thorn's cell phone alarm woke her. She checked the time to see it was six-thirty. Groggy, she hurried to her bathroom to rub the sleepies from her eyes and brush her hair. On second consideration, she twisted off the cap to her mouthwash to take a swig. She spit out the bright green liquid before leaving her room and finding Thorn tying on his boots.

"I didn't mean to wake you," he said and got to his feet.

"That's okay."

He smiled at her from where he stood. "You look cute in pajamas."

Blushing, she looked down at her feet and tugged on the hem of her top. "Thanks." She peered at him again. "Do you have time for coffee?"

"Of course."

They drank coffee together in the silence of the early morning. Seeing him sitting across from her gave her hope that one day this would be normal. She wanted that. More than anything.

"If you don't want to go out tonight, I'd understand," Thorn said suddenly.

She had forgotten about their dinner date after everything that had happened. "No, I want to." She studied the dark surface of her coffee. "I'm not going to let Damon win anymore."

A smile flickered on his lips, and she thought about their kiss last night.

"I should get going." He set his coffee cup in the sink.

At the front door, Amanda stood with him.

"I'm looking forward to tonight," he said.

"Me, too."

He hesitated before kissing her on the cheek. "See you later."

"Bye."

She stayed there a moment while he walked to his car. When he got in, she waved her hand in the air and then closed the door. A smile played a happy tune on her lips. In the kitchen, she washed their cups and set them side by side on the drying rack.

****

At work, Beth came up to her with a cautious look in her eyes, as if she were afraid of saying or doing the wrong thing. “Are you okay?”

“Yeah. I’m fine.” Amanda fiddled with her fingers. “I’m sorry for what Damon did.”

“Let me stop you right there.” Beth held up a hand. “You don’t have to apologize for a damn thing that man does. You’re not responsible for him. Fact is, I’m not worried about him. I’m worried about you. So…are you really okay?”

Amanda nodded. “I asked Thorn to stay…the night.”

Beth’s eyes widened. “You what?”

“Nothing happened,” she replied quickly.

“I didn’t ask if it did.”

Amanda pointed. “Yeah, but that look in your eye was wondering.”

Beth smirked.

“He slept on the couch.” Amanda shrugged. “Nights are hard. I didn’t want to be alone.”

“I get it. I’m glad he could be there for you.”

“Tonight is our date.” Amanda bit her bottom lip. “I don’t have anything to wear.”

Beth let out a laugh. “Leave that to Leighton.”

During their lunch break, Beth took Amanda to Leighton’s boutique. The mannequins wore dresses of lace and silk, with interesting shapes and necklines, beaded and ruffled, solid colors and loud patterns. The racks contained even more. So many options of varying lengths and styles. Amanda was relieved she didn’t have to choose one herself.

“What about this?” Leighton held up a red dress with cutouts that would reveal a lot of skin, especially of Amanda's stomach.

"I cannot wear that."

"Why not?" Leighton pouted. "I'd wear it on a date with Thorn."

"Exactly," Beth said. "You'd wear it, but this dress is for Amanda."

Leighton scrutinized the dress. "Right. All wrong for Amanda. So, what kind of dress are you comfortable wearing?"

Amanda shrugged. "Something simple."

"I prefer the term 'classic.' I have a lot of classic sundresses and cocktail dresses. You should definitely wear an A-line dress. Show off your legs a bit. It's also more laid-back, perfect for a first date to a nice restaurant. Do you know where he's taking you?"

"No."

"That's all right. I have dresses that could work for any setting." She circled, scanning the racks with her professional eye. "Would you be comfortable in a pencil dress or a skirt with shape and movement?"

"Um. The latter." Having men stare at her body, lusting after her curves, made her uncomfortable. Wearing a dress would already be a step outside of her comfort zone, but a tight-fitting one would only add to that.

"What about neckline and sleeves?"

Amanda bit her bottom lip. For the Christmas party, her dress had quarter sleeves and a hemline that came a couple of inches past her knees in the front and became longer in the back. She'd felt beautiful and confident in it. "Nothing too…revealing."

Leighton nodded. "No worries." She headed to a rack. "The dresses in my shop would look stunning on you, but here's one that I think fits your needs." The black dress on the hanger had a scoop neck, short-sleeves, and a skirt that flared. It was perfect. Not flashy. Not revealing. Because she didn't wear dresses, it wouldn't be boring. "I have it in a few colors. Black, white, cobalt, maroon, and eggplant." She picked up each one as she listed the colors. "What do you think?"

Amanda considered the options. "Color is good."

"Yes, it is." Leighton put the black and white dresses back. One at time, she held up the other three dresses in front of Amanda. Beth stood back to take a look. "What do you think?" Leighton asked Beth.

"They all work great with her coloring."

Leighton nodded. "What do you think, sweetie? There's a mirror behind you." She handed the dresses to Amanda.

Amanda studied her reflection with each dress in front of her. All three of the colors were beautiful, but one color stood out. "This one. Thorn likes blue."

Beth and Leighton nodded.

"The cobalt will look stunning on you," Leighton said.

"Thorn will love it," Beth added.

Leighton winked. "Yes, he will."

Amanda's face warmed. She hoped he would.

After work, Beth and Leighton flocked to Amanda's house to help her get ready. Leighton unloaded an arsenal of beauty and hair supplies. She used a wide curling iron on Amanda's hair while Beth stood back watching the process.

"What's your beauty specialty?" Amanda asked Beth.

"Mine? I have none," Beth said. "I'm a lip balm

kind of girl, but I can manage minimal makeup. If I were to touch Leighton's makeup, though, she'd slap my hands."

"Damn right I would." Leighton wound a chunk of Amanda's hair around the hot iron. "Don't worry. I've got you, girl. When Thorn sees you, he'll be stunned speechless."

Chapter Nine

Thorn stood outside a restaurant, on the sidewalk near the door. He wore dark wash jeans—because he'd feel like a fraud in trousers—a white button-down shirt, and a black dinner jacket. Only Donovan knew Thorn didn't own a dinner jacket, because the jacket in question belonged to Donovan. Thorn had stopped by after work to pick it up. When he did, Donovan cracked a joke about Thorn really wanting to impress Amanda. Thorn told him to shut up, but added another choice word in there, before leaving with the jacket over his arm.

Now he waited nervously for Amanda. Since she hadn't sent him a text to back out, he hoped that meant their date was on track. He'd waited so long for this evening that all day he kept pinching himself. Hard. The pain never woke him. Still, his heart raced. For Amanda, he wanted this date to go well. She deserved to know what it felt like to be wined and dined, treated right, and he wanted to be the man to give her that.

He rubbed his hands together. Restlessness had his leg muscles twitching and his feet shifting, but he rooted in place to stop himself from pacing. Couples walked past him, entering and leaving the restaurant. He diverted his gaze from them, because seeing their smiling faces and affection for each other was increasing his anxiety.

The sound of heels clicking on the sidewalk caught his attention. He turned and couldn't stop himself from gawking. Amanda looked stunning with her hair like sunshine in waves around her face, candy pink lips, a blue dress that swished gently around her thighs, and high heels in the same pink as her lipstick.

Amanda came to a halt and peered down at her feet. "Is something wrong?"

"What?" He jumped. "No. Not at all. You're gorgeous. I'm sorry for staring. I was thinking about how beautiful you are."

She smiled. "Thank you. And you look quite dashing yourself."

"I tried."

"You pulled it off."

He held out his arm to her. "Hungry?"

"Very." She accepted his arm, and he opened the door to the restaurant.

The maître d' seated them at a table with a white tablecloth and a small glass bowl with candles floating in water that cast flickers of light onto the table. Thorn did the gentlemanly thing he'd been told to do and pulled out her chair. Her perfume lingered in the air a moment when she sat down. He inhaled it while she scooted closer to the table. As he walked to his side, she laid the linen napkin in her lap and took the menu from the maître d'.

He thanked their host when he took his own menu. Then the two of them looked over their menus quietly for a moment. Thorn struggled to pay attention to the options, though, with Amanda sitting so gorgeously across from him.

"Would it be tacky of me to order a beer?"

Amanda asked.

Thorn looked up. “I have no idea whether it would be considered tacky or not, but my personal opinion…hell no. I’d find it sexy.”

She blushed, making her look even prettier. “Good because I’m not much of a wine person. I like beer.”

My kind of girl.

A waiter came over to get their drink orders. “For you, ma’am?”

“Sierra Nevada.”

A craft beer to boot. Damn she is one of a kind.

“Very good, and you, sir?”

“Same.”

“Do you need any more time to look over the menu?”

Thorn looked to Amanda.

“I’m ready to order now,” she said. “I’d like the rib-eye steak. Medium, please.”

Thorn chuckled. “Actually, same again, but rare for me.”

When the waiter left, Thorn said, “You’re a girl after my heart.”

She laughed but probably didn’t know she’d had his heart for a long time. She didn’t know because he hadn’t told her. Telling her before now would’ve been disastrous. He needed to wait. How long? He didn’t know, but he’d been waiting this long already, so he’d continue to wait for however much longer was necessary.

While they waited for their food, they talked and sipped their beers. Amanda appeared at ease, and he loved that. He sure hoped he appeared as calm on the outside as she did.

"May I ask you a question?" Amanda said.

"Of course."

She reached across the table and tapped her nail onto the tablecloth in front of his ring finger. "Can you tell me about your ring?"

Thorn curled his fingers into his palm. "This ring belonged to my father. He died in the line of duty, and my mother gave me his ring to honor him. I didn't wear it until she died, to honor them both. Also, I heard that wearing a ring at work keeps the crazies at bay."

"Does it work?"

"Not really. I get hit on a lot because the women are too drunk or high to notice."

She covered her face as she laughed. "I'm sorry, that's not funny."

"And yet you're still laughing."

A snort escaped her, and he joined in her laughter.

"But seriously, though," she said when she controlled herself, "wearing your father's ring is incredibly sweet." She fooled with the napkin in her lap. "I have one more question…if that's okay."

"I'll answer any questions you have."

Her lips spread into a wide smile. "What's your first name?"

Out of all the questions she could've asked him, he didn't expect that one. He grinned. Wanting to know his first name made sense.

"Nicholas, but family and friends from school call me Nick."

"Nick Thorn." She tried out his full name for the first time. "I like it, but do you want me to call you Nick from now on?"

"No, you can call me Thorn. Everyone does. It's

kind of stuck."

Her smile grew. "I like calling you Thorn."

He gazed into her eyes. "I like hearing you call me Thorn."

Their gazes locked for several seconds, and then the waiter interrupted their connection when he set their plates in front of them. Their food gave them the perfect reason to sink into silence for a moment while they cut into and tasted their steaks. He worried that admitting he liked hearing her say his name might've been too much for her to handle, but he wanted her to know the truth. Their relationship had started so slowly and cautiously, that a mere flicker of eye contact, a tentative smile, her asking him a question, giving a shy "hello," or saying his name had invigorated him.

"Are you an only child?" Amanda asked.

He sawed off a neat square of meat. "Yeah. I am now. I mean…when I was nine, my three-year-old sister passed away from leukemia."

Amanda's mouthed opened, and her wide eyes reflected heartbreak. "I'm so sorry."

"Thanks." He stared at the cube of beef speared onto the end of his fork. "I guess that's why I've adopted Beth as my little sister…to fill that hole."

She tilted her head. "That's sweet."

"I believe we attract the people we need in life. I needed Beth to take over my sister's long-vacant place, Donovan needed me when he lost Ryan, and they needed each other."

"And I needed…*need*…you to fill the hole…*holes*…Damon created."

Thorn stared at Amanda. His heart beat double-time. Her feeling comfortable enough to reveal that and the strides they'd made recently boosted his confidence. The fact they were having dinner together in a romantic setting, out in public, proved they'd come a long way. He looked forward to going the full distance with her.

"I need you, too," he said.

Amanda's chest rose and fell rapidly. She didn't look away from him. His own chest constricted. He didn't want this moment to get any heavier. If it continued, he feared she'd pull back into her shell.

"Do you have any siblings?"

She nodded and resumed cutting her steak. "Two sisters. One older, one younger. They tried to get me away from Damon, but when he threatened to kill them, I cut all ties. For their safety."

"Do they know you're living in Florida?"

"When I moved, I never told them or my parents where I went, in case Damon ever tried to threaten them for information about me."

Thorn nodded. That made sense. Many women harbored the real and understandable fear that their abusers would find them again, would use their loved ones against them. For Amanda, that fear wasn't just realistic but happening.

"But when he left his first note at my house," Amanda continued, "I called them to say he found me and I'd keep them updated. I didn't tell them much more, like where I worked, to be on the safe side." She sighed. "I miss them so much. I didn't contact them for years because, for all I knew, he was watching them. That's why they couldn't visit me here, in case he followed. And that's why I couldn't go back there to see them." Her fingers picked at the napkin in her lap. "I was too afraid of running into him."

"One day, you'll be able to see them again."

Amanda took a deep breath. "I hope so."

"I know so. It'll happen."

She lowered her gaze. "Thanks."

They finished their dinners and lingered over coffee while talking and getting to know each other. By the end of the evening, Thorn was content, but he didn't want their date to come to a close. Hands in his pockets, he walked Amanda to her car. She pulled the keys out of her purse and unlocked the door. He held it open for her, so she could climb in, but before she did, she faced him. Her hand molded around his shoulder, and she leaned in. Her lips pressed against his cheek so quickly he wouldn't have noticed if it weren't for the tingle on his skin. Then she stood back, looking shy, but she didn't move her hand from his shoulder.

Staring at him, she stepped closer. She got close enough that their noses brushed. He held her hips carefully, not wanting to startle her. When he did, though, she shifted her hips into his.

Their lips connected.

He kissed her with care, wanting her to feel as cherished as she deserved to be, but also not overwhelm her with demanding too much too soon. The kiss stretched on. He enjoyed the texture of her lips and the lingering flavors of steak, beer, and coffee. With his lips, he committed hers to memory—their shape and suppleness. It was all he could've asked for, the perfect conclusion.

"Thank you for tonight," she whispered. "We should do it again."

He grinned. "Tell me when and where, and I'll be there."

"Bye."

"Bye. Drive safely."

"I will." She slipped into the driver's seat, and he shut the door for her.

He stood on the sidewalk while she pulled out of the parking space. Through the window, he saw her wave at him. He waved back. When she drove toward the exit, he went to his car, unable to stop himself from beaming from ear to ear. Sitting in his car, he beat his hands against the steering wheel in an excited tempo. The date had gone better than he'd imagined it would. Every moment of it. Seeing Amanda sitting across from him somewhere that was not The Fighting Chance hadn't felt real to him. Once, he had even pinched himself when she wasn't looking, to make sure he wasn't hallucinating.

During his drive home, he couldn't stop smiling, couldn't get how beautiful she looked out of his head. The scent of her perfume continued to swim in his nostrils. He arrived home high on the events of the evening, especially that kiss. Man, *that* kiss.

After a fast shower and downing a glass of water, he sat down on the edge of his bed. His phone buzzed when he reached toward the bedside lamp. He picked up his phone and read the text from Amanda.

Goodnight.

Her courage in texting him before going to bed didn't escape him. Smiling, he fired off a text in reply. *Sweet dreams.*

He didn't know what the next day would bring, but he looked forward to it. Lying in the darkness, he thought about Amanda in her bed miles away. He hoped she felt as happy as he did in that moment, because he'd never felt happier.

Chapter Ten

Banging noises woke Amanda from a sound sleep. She launched into a sitting position with her arms out, ready to fend off an attacker. The bang came again. She snatched up her cell phone and scrambled out of bed. Her hands shook as she unlocked her bedroom door. Another bang. She ran toward it. At the hall to her front door, her feet skid to a stop. Her front door vibrated in its frame from vicious beatings. The bolts and chains held on for dear life. Another hit had the door quaking.

She spun on her heels and dashed into the kitchen where she opened the cabinet door beneath the counter. On her hands and knees, she crawled into the small space. After she'd moved into this house, she had had the wood divider that separated the double-door cabinet separated from the single-door cabinet. One day, she knew she'd have to hide, and not many people thought to check kitchen cabinets while searching for someone, because usually they were too small. The extended bottom cabinet fit her, with her legs bent, and nothing else occupied the space. Not a single pot or pan.

She pulled the cabinet door shut and pressed the Home button on her phone. The bright screen blinded her in the darkness. Squinting, she swiped her finger over the device to lower the screen's glare. As soon as it dimmed, she tapped in her passcode and called Thorn. All the while, the banging at her front door didn’t cease. It wouldn’t be able to hold up to much more abuse.

Thorn answered on the second ring. “Amanda, what’s—”

“He’s here,” she whispered, cutting off his question. “He’s trying to break down my door. I’m hiding in a kitchen cabinet.”

“I’m on my way. I’ll be there as fast as I can.”

A bang echoed through her house.

“I’m scared.”

“I know, baby. I’m coming. Put your phone on silent. I need to hang up to call this in and get backup. I’ll call you right back.”

“Okay.”

The line went dead.

She quickly changed her ringtone to silent.

A boom shook her house with the crack of wood. Her front door lost.

Heavy boots pounded tile. “Amanda!”

His voice, calling out her name in a roar of anger. She’d heard it many times before, every time she’d try to hide from him. He’d scream her name like that on the other side of their bathroom door, as she quivered in a ball at the bottom of the bathtub.

“Amanda!”

Her phone buzzed in her hand. She answered it right away and held it to her ear. “He’s…in.” Her words were little more than a breath.

“Put your phone on speaker. I won’t say a word, but I need to hear what happens.”

Hands trembling, she did as he asked and held the phone’s speaker toward the cabinet door. Her body shivered. Fear made her not want to breathe. If she did,

Damon would find her.

"Amanda!"

Something crashed.

"I know you're here, you fucking whore. I saw you tonight. I saw you with *him*. In his arms. Kissing him!"

Glass shattered.

Amanda covered her mouth with her free hand.

"I'm going to find you, and when I do, I'm going to make it perfectly clear you're mine. No one else's. Not his. Not any man's. Mine!"

His thundering footsteps headed toward her bedroom. Thumping sounds escaped her bedroom as he tore it apart hunting for her. She imagined him checking in all the places she used to hide before, in all the places he'd find her—under the bed, in the corner of the closet, in the bathroom. Any nook or cranny where she used to tremor and plead with him to leave her alone.

Glass broke.

Seconds later, he returned.

"After I deal with you, I'm going to find him and kill him. I'm going to rip out his tongue for kissing you! You hear that, Amanda?"

The door to the garage whammed into the wall. Her car doors banged. The trunk made a boom when he slammed it down.

"Where the fuck are you? I know you're here." The sound of his growling voice caused her to shrink in fear.

Thuds came from the living room. All of a sudden, there was an explosion of thick glass and a thundering clatter of metal. She jumped inside the cabinet, realizing he'd broken her sliding glass door.

"Amanda!" His roar became monstrous. Demonic.

His rage was monumental. If he found her now, he wouldn't only make her pay with bruises and broken bones. He'd kill her.

He stomped into the kitchen. The contents in the refrigerator door rattled when he yanked it open. A yell ripped from his throat, and several things pummeled the floor. Bottles rolled noisily. For a moment, all was silent. Then the gentle *whoosh* of a beer bottle cap being twisted off met her ears. He gulped it down. All the times he'd knock back beers rushed back to her.

Drunk Damon was even more ruthless. Alcohol fueled him, encouraged him.

Glass smashed against the tile. Pieces pelted into the cabinet doors.

The oven door squealed. Damon rammed it shut. The metallic bang which followed jostled the pans in the drawer beneath the oven.

"Amanda!"

Above her head, the counter boomed. The cabinet door in front of her bounced against the wooden frame and swung out slightly. She flinched from it, pressing her back into the wood panel behind her. Through the crack, she eyed Damon's pant leg. He stood over her and didn't even know it. If he looked down and saw the cabinet door open, would he look? Would he find her?

She held her breath.

Damon's voice reached her. This time, though, he wasn't yelling. He was growling beneath this voice, talking to himself, making a vow. "I'll find you, Amanda, and you'll finally learn your lesson."

His lessons had always involved blood and bruises.

She swallowed and closed her eyes.

More crashes as Damon swept the contents of the

countertops to the floor. The destruction moved back into the living room. Slowly, it made its way to her bedroom.

Glass.

Hammering.

Beating.

Furniture toppling.

Fabric ripping.

Sirens.

Damon's laughter.

"You think they can stop me? Oh, no, Amanda. They can't stop me. No one can. I'll be back. You have my word. I'll be back for you."

Silence.

Amanda gripped the phone to her chest, too afraid to speak in case Damon hadn't actually left and was waiting for her to leave her hiding place, waiting to snatch her and haul her out of there before the police could arrive. She shuddered while trying to keep her body still. A leg reacting to scared reflexes could knock a knee or foot against a solid surface, giving her away.

The sirens were right outside now.

Several car doors slammed.

"This is the Orlando Police Department," a voice she didn't recognize shouted.

Shuffling sounded.

"Clear."

"Clear."

"Clear."

Silence.

"Amanda, baby, you can come out."

Thorn.

"He's not here. You're safe now." Thorn's voice

came from a few feet away.

She pushed open the cabinet door. Thorn stood in the middle of the kitchen's carnage—coffee mug shards, chunks of glass from her blender, broken bottles and puddles of beer, busted condiment bottles, spewing Ketchup, sweet dill relish, and soy sauce.

"Amanda." Thorn rushed to her. Glass crunched beneath his shoes. He squatted down to help her out of the cabinet. Once on her feet, she threw her arms around him. He held her close. "I've got you," he whispered in her ear.

And she always wanted him to have her. She never wanted him to let go.

A police officer stepped into the kitchen. "Detective, a word?"

Thorn pulled away from her. He brought a chair over and set it down where she stood. "Don't move until I can get you shoes."

She nodded and lowered onto the chair.

Thorn went over to where a few officers had congregated. They spoke to him in hushed tones. Thorn's body was tense and didn't relax. He left their circle and went to her bedroom. A minute later, he returned with a pair of sneakers and socks.

She took them, and he squatted in front of her. Before he could speak, she said, "I already know. They couldn't find him." She pulled the socks on. "He's good at that." It was what he always did; escape the police, flee justice. She shoved her feet into the sneakers.

"I will get him, Amanda."

Her heart shook. "Unless he gets you first."

His jaw ticked. No doubt, he had things to say about that. He was in law enforcement, after all, but she knew Damon. He didn't.

She got to her feet and made her way through the trashed kitchen. In the living room, Damon had tossed the couch cushions left and right. A dining room chair lay atop giant shards of glass from the sliding glass door. A large dent in the hurricane shutters showed where the chair had collided into it. Her booby traps had been demolished, too. Those wouldn't fool Damon now. Her bookcase lay on its belly, with books crushed beneath its weight.

Her bedroom wasn't any better. Damon had chucked the mattress and box spring off the frame to the other side of the room. Her bedside lamp was smashed on the floor. Her clothes had been ripped from the hangers and strewn here and there. In the bathroom, he'd driven a fist into the mirror. The shower curtain rod had been yanked from its perch and tossed into the tub. The curtain itself was a tangle of plastic.

Sitting on her reconstructed couch, she told the officers what had happened. Thorn corroborated her story, having heard everything.

"We'll board up your house, and a car will stay out front to make sure he doesn't return. Do you have someone you can stay with tonight?"

"She does," Thorn said. "I'll take her."

Amanda packed a bag with a change of clothes and a few toiletries. On the walk to her front door, she noticed the sliding glass door had been covered with a sheet of plywood. Once she was outside, the officers nailed wood over her ruined front door and placed police tape across it. She imagined it'd look that way if they'd found her dead body among the kitchen wreckage. Thorn escorted her to the front passenger seat of his car. Immediately, her body broke down. She began to quiver uncontrollably. Hating this sign of weakness, she wrapped her hands around the seat belt across her chest and gave it a death grip. Her legs shook. She pressed the back of her head into the headrest and squeezed her eyelids shut. Nothing could stop her body from reacting to the adrenaline let-down.

"Amanda, I want to do something to comfort you, but I don't know what you wouldn't want me to do." His caution tugged at her heart. All she wanted was his arms around her, but since he was driving, that wasn't possible. So, she took the hand he rested on the gear shift and placed it on her leg, near her knee. He automatically squeezed her leg. She drew what she needed from that contact, letting it fill her with strength. Slowly, her shaking lessened to occasional shivers, and her breathing came easier.

With her eyes finally open, she realized they weren't headed in the direction of Beth and Donovan's house, as she had expected. "Where are we going? This isn't the way to Beth's house."

"I'm not taking you there. We're going to my place."

She inhaled and exhaled. A million thoughts swirled in her head.

"I should've asked, but after what happened…what I heard…I want to be close to you."

She swallowed. "It's okay. I want to be close to you, too."

His left hand tightened around the steering wheel, but the other kept the same amount of pressure on her leg. In that moment, she wanted to do so many things. She yearned to ask him to pull over so she could kiss him, but she didn't. She tamped down the urge to tell him how much she wanted him and how much that scared her.

Her thoughts squawked at her like a chicken again.

Oh, give me a break! You know what I just went through, for goodness' sake.

Thorn pulled up to a house with a large oak tree in the front. The evergreen trim and neat row of Emerald Green Arborvitae growing alongside the driveway suited him. She gripped the handles of her duffel bag in front of her as Thorn unlocked the door. He let her in first. She stepped in, jittering with nerves.

The walls were painted a soft beige. For a man in law enforcement, and a bachelor to boot, his place looked much homier than hers did. A dark brown suede couch, large flat-screen TV, and framed photographs of the Grand Canyon gave his home a warmth that matched what he exuded every day.

"Your place is great."

"Thank you. And, please, make yourself at home."

She set her duffle bag on the floor next to the couch. "Do you happen to have any alcohol here?"

He smiled. "Ycah." He poured them a couple fingers of whiskey.

The first swallow filled her with heat, from her throat to her stomach. They drank in silence, sitting on the couch with a cushion between them. After they finished the amber liquid, Thorn put their glasses away.

"You should get some sleep," he said.

She diverted her gaze.

"I'll sleep on the couch," he added.

"No, you—"

He cut her off. "I will sleep on the couch. Not

you."

She smiled. "That's not what I was going to say." Now she stared at her hands. "I don't know how to even ask this."

"What is it?"

Avoiding his gaze, she said with a soft voice, "Can I…sleep…beside you?" She peeked at him when he didn't respond. "Never mind. It's a big ask."

"No. It's not. If you'd be comfortable, we can do that."

"I would be."

Nerves ricocheted inside her when she stepped into his bedroom, a place she'd never been. This space matched him, too, with the black comforter, dark oak furniture, and forest green paint. After she kicked off her shoes, she climbed into his bed, beneath the comforter. His scent surrounded her, making her light-headed. She turned onto her side, so she wouldn't be able to see Thorn.

A knock sounded.

"Can I come in?"

He'd let her go into his room without him.

"Yeah."

He moved quietly.

The light switched off.

The other side of the bed shifted as he lay down.

She held still, aware of how close Thorn was. Her entire body hummed with the knowledge. She gripped the pillow she cuddled to her head. *Too soon. Too soon.* After what happened, with the fear Damon had inflicted on the forefront of her mind, it was too soon to do anything more with Thorn.

"Thank you," she said into the darkness.

"For what?"

"For not thinking I wanted to do something else. Other men would've assumed."

"I'm not like other men."

"No, you're not, and I thank God for that." She turned over and scooted closer. He lifted his arm, allowing her to tuck herself into his side. "Goodnight, Thorn."

He kissed her temple. "Goodnight, Amanda."

Chapter Eleven

Thorn closed his eyes, relishing the feel of Amanda in his arms. He'd wanted her there for so long. God, he'd always wanted to hold her, make her feel safe and secure. His heart ached with it at times, especially during the moments when she retreated from him. In this moment, though, his heart pounded with relief. He held her tighter.

Throughout the night, their arms stayed around each other, even if they changed positions. He often woke up, worried she'd be gone, something he'd hallucinated in the night, out of his exhaustion and deepest desires. But she was real. She was there.

When the room lightened with the rising sun, turning the sky into shades of gray, he stared at the back of her head, in awe of the way the light changed the tone of her blonde hair. She let out a soft sigh and turned her head toward him. Her eyes were still closed, and he admired her face—the slope of her nose, the shape and color of her lips, the way her lashes curled against her skin, the strokes of her cheekbones and jaw. Sleep settled her face into serene lines she often didn't have while awake and on alert. He yearned to trace her features with his fingers, to touch her hair. He wanted to marvel at her beauty, openly, not in secret.

She let out a long exhale, and her lashes parted. Her gaze met his. She didn't flinch at seeing him awake and staring at her. Instead, she stared back, unabashed.

He didn't say a word but studied her in the silence punctuated by their breathing. *She's so damn stunning.* He couldn't imagine ever raising a hand to hurt her. Nor would he ever. How could any man want to hurt a woman? To bruise? Scar? The thought sickened him. And Damon had done that to her repeatedly. The bastard had wanted to do that to her last night. Worse.

Amanda turned onto her side and slid to him until her body was flush against his, surprising him. She laid a hand on his face and pressed her lips to his. When she eased back, her hand remained on his cheek, and she scanned his eyes, searching for something. He didn't know what. Then she kissed him again. This time, her lips molded around his top lip, sucking gently.

His hand cupped her hip. As their kiss stretched on, he slipped his hand to her back, edging her closer. Even though he didn't want it to, for Amanda's sake, his body reacted to having her pressed against him, as well as from the kiss. He started to shift back so she wouldn't be uncomfortable, but her leg hooked around his, keeping him in place. And she inched closer. The contact electrified him. Urges exploded through his body. He wanted her. Oh, damn, did he want her, but he wished to take things slow. Except she was so pliant and warm. So responsive. He struggled to pull back. Whenever they came to be intimate, he didn't want her to regret it. If she did, he'd hate himself for it.

A moan floated from her lips.

His own moan responded.

Their hormones were ready—screaming ready—but were their brains?

Thorn's alarm went off, startling them. He turned

over and killed the racket. Lying on his back, he panted. Next to him, Amanda breathed deeply.

“I think I’m going to need a cold shower,” he said to the ceiling.

Amanda laughed. “Me, too.” She fell silent a moment. “I’ll go find something to make for breakfast. Take your time.” She crawled out of the bed, and he watched her go. In her cotton pajamas, she was incredibly cute.

He took the coldest shower he could bear for as long as he could tolerate it. When his hormones finally got their shit together, he shaved and dressed. He came out of the bedroom to the smell of bacon and eggs. In the kitchen, Amanda flipped an omelet. Seeing her there, cooking as if it was normal, made him smile. He joined her. “Do you need any help?”

“Nope. The omelets and bacon are done, and the toast should be popping up soon.”

“This is a better breakfast than I’ve had in a long time. I’ve gotten pretty lazy about it.”

“Well, I figured I owed you for putting up with me last night.” She smiled.

“You say that as if it was an imposition.”

She peered at him. “Wasn’t it?”

“Far from it.”

She lowered her gaze as she placed cheese omelets on two plates. “Thanks for saying that.”

He took the hot skillet from her and set it aside. “It’s the truth, Amanda. I will do anything for you. I don’t just care about you, I—”

The toast popped up.

He swallowed. Was it too soon to tell her his true feelings? Would it terrify her if he did? He lifted the toast out and began to butter them. "It's not just an attraction," he muttered. "And it's not because protecting others is in my DNA. It's so much more than that."

"I know," she whispered.

Out of the corner of his eye, he saw her dividing up the crisp bacon; they had to occupy their hands and minds while revealing these things to each other.

"What I feel for you, I haven't felt before," she admitted. "I certainly never felt this way with…*him*…not even in the beginning. I had no chance to. But after what I've put you through…this tug-of-war…and with Damon being here now, I wonder if one day it'll be too much for you and you'll…" Her voice trailed off.

Thorn turned to her. He took her arms so she faced him, too. "I'll say it a thousand times. And a thousand more times after that. I'll always say it…that's not going to happen. I'm not going to leave. I'm not going to desert you. I'm not going to abuse you. I'm not going to give up on you. I'm—"

She silenced him with her lips. The kiss was deep. This time, with tongue. Her mouth tasted like mint. He had the briefest thought that she must've brushed her teeth in the guest bathroom while he showered, but it didn't matter. All that mattered was what she gave him through that kiss. She kissed him with such gratitude that it struck him in the gut; she believed him. That wasn't easy for her. Not after Damon had used words to manipulate her in the past.

A phone sounded with an incoming call.

"Is it me, or is something always interrupting us?" Amanda said.

He chuckled softly. "I think it's your phone this time."

She pulled away from him. "It's Beth. I had texted her about what happened last night." She answered the call. "Hey, Beth."

Thorn listened to one side of the conversation.

"I'm okay. I swear I'm okay. The police got there before he could find me… Yes, I called Thorn. He was there… I'm with him now…" She turned her back to him and whispered, "We will talk about that later."

Thorn smirked.

"No, you don't have to do that… No, Beth…" She let out a huff. "Okay, fine… Okay. Thank you… Yeah, we'll see you in a bit. Bye."

She smiled at him. "Beth is closing The Fighting Chance today. She won't hear any objections to it. She and Donovan want to come over to my house and be there with me and help me to clean up and make sure…that I'm safe…"

"I want that, too."

They ate their breakfast, lost in their own thoughts, and then Thorn drove Amanda home. The closer they got to her house, the tenser she became. A cop car waited out front when he pulled into the driveway. He went down to speak to the officer while Amanda sat in the car.

He showed the officer his badge. "I'm bringing Amanda back home. Was there any activity during the night? Any sign of Damon Hunter?"

"None. It was quiet."

"Thank you for your vigilance." He went back to the car. "It's okay," he told Amanda. "He didn't come back."

She pulled her keys from her purse and pushed the portable garage door opener. “Since the door is boarded, we can go through the garage.” The door lifted, revealing her car and a bunch of cardboard boxes that cluttered half of the two-car garage. She unlocked and opened the door to a waft of foul air.

“Oh, no.” Groaning, she covered her nose and mouth with her hand. “The mess in the kitchen.”

Thorn helped her open the windows to air out the house with cross ventilation. It didn’t make a dent in the odor, but it would eventually. Beth and Donovan arrived a few minutes later with the twins. They walked through the house speechlessly. Donovan wore his “I-need-to-kick-someone’s-ass” face, a face Thorn knew well. Beth had on her “I-need-to-kick-someone’s-ass” face, too, but there was also horror. A man had done this while searching for her friend, a woman who she’d taught self-defense for years. It wasn’t an easy thing to see. In the light of day, the destruction was even more visible, and it punched him in the gut.

“Where were you hiding?’ Beth asked, with Reagan on her hip.

Amanda pointed at the opened kitchen cabinet. “It’s one of my hiding places.”

Beth nodded. “You’re smart.”

“Paranoid is more like it.” Amanda glanced at Thorn. “But it came in handy.”

Thorn rubbed her back.

“Has Damon been spotted anywhere?” Donovan asked.

Thorn shook his head. “No.” He stole a peek at Amanda, regretting that fact.

“If you need my help, just ask.”

"Thanks, Donovan." He checked his watch. "I wish I could stay, but I have to go." Off to the side, he stroked Amanda's arms. "I'll come by during my lunch break and offer a hand."

"The twins will keep me safe in the meantime," Amanda said.

He smiled. "I'm a phone call away."

"I know." She placed a hand over her heart. "That's why I still keep your business card here."

Knowing that, Thorn hooked a finger under her chin and pressed his mouth to hers. But with Beth and Donovan a few feet away, watching out of the corner of their eyes, he didn't escalate the kiss into anything more than a simple touch of lips. On the way out, he told Beth under his breath, "Take care of her."

Beth nodded. "We will."

He had every faith they would.

At work, Thorn went to Officer Burnett, the same officer who had assisted when Buck, one of Ryan Goldwyn's murderers, was at large. He'd been there for Donovan, and last night, he had been one of the officers on the scene. Thorn had called him directly.

"Hey, Burnett."

"Hey, Thorn."

"Any news on Damon Hunter?"

With his hands on his hips, above his utility belt, Burnett shook his head. "I've been trying, man. I went to several of the closest hotels and motels to Amanda's house last night and spoke to the managers or front desk receptionists. He didn't have a room with any of them, but there are a lot of establishments he could be staying at. I also looked up his DMV records. He's registered with a black 2019 Ram 1500 Laramie. A truck like that isn't hard to spot, but no one has seen it. A truck of that description wasn't even caught leaving Amanda's neighborhood last night."

"He could be driving something less conspicuous," Thorn said.

"If he wants to stay close to her, unseen…I'm guessing so."

"Damn it."

"We'll find him, Thorn," Burnett tried to reassure him.

"Before or after he tries to kill her again?"

"We're doing everything we can."

Thorn raked his hands through his hair. "I know."

Burnett cocked his head to the side. "I saw how you were with her last night. You're in a relationship with her, aren't you?"

"It's more than that." Thorn slipped his hands into his pockets. "I'm in love with her."

Burnett nodded. "Should you be working this case?"

Thorn glared at him. "No one, not even Chief Cormac, would be able to take me off."

"All right. Look, I'll help you in any way I can."

"Thanks. I appreciate that."

Thorn sat down at his desk and began to make phone calls to contact the hotels and motels Burnett hadn't gone to within a five-mile radius of Amanda's house. It made sense that Damon would be close enough to spy on Amanda whenever he desired, and to get to her house quickly when he got the urge to see her or make her pay for an imaginary slight. He spent hours on the phone to be told time and time again that no one under the name of Damon Hunter had checked in. The faxes he sent of Damon's mugshot from a couple years ago also didn't yield any results.

Frustrated, he hung up his phone and guzzled water from a bottle. His throat was dry, and his patience was running out. Where was the bastard? As far as Thorn could tell, he wasn't staying at a hotel, or motel, or bed and breakfast, not even up to eight miles out, which could mean Damon stayed mobile, possibly sleeping in a car. That method would have Damon close to Amanda, no matter the time of day or night. Thorn wouldn't put it past the man who had followed Amanda to and from work every day.

During his lunch break, Thorn drove straight to Amanda's. First, he canvassed the neighborhood, driving slowly, looking for any signs of Damon and any vehicles acting suspicious. A cable company truck was parked at the end of the road in front of a house, but unless Damon got a job working for a cable company in Florida and made sure his calls put him in Amanda's neighborhood, Thorn doubted that was him.

He pulled up to Amanda's house. Two vans sat in the driveway, and a man stood in the doorway, repairing the splintered doorframe. Another set of men came around the side from the backyard, carrying chunks of the broken sliding glass door to the open back end of one of the vans. Thorn waved at them and thanked the man at the entrance as he stepped inside.

The rotten smell had greatly diminished. Only a hint of it hung in the air. The glass had been swept away, too, and everything set right.

Amanda sat on the floor with Ryan in front of her. She rolled a small rubber ball to him, causing him to break out into giggles. Beth and Donovan occupied the couch. Reagan gripped Donovan's fingers and bounced up and down on the couch cushion between him and Beth. Seeing them like that, having fun and bonding in a house that hadn't experienced much of that, where last night things could've turned into a tragedy, made him smile.

Amanda looked up at him when he entered. Her face lit up even more. "Hey."

"Hey," he said. "It looks good in here."

She glanced around. The workers had removed the hurricane shutters so they could get to the sliding glass door. Right now, nothing separated the house from the porch. Sunlight streamed inside, and wind blew through the living room. The booby traps in front of the doors and windows had also been dismantled. It looked like a normal home. Albeit missing a couple doors.

"It does," she said.

Thorn sat down on the floor next to her. She passed him the small plastic ball, and he bounced it toward Ryan, who laughed so hard he tipped backward. Thorn and Amanda launched forward and caught the toddler with a hand on his back. Shoulder to shoulder, each of them supporting Ryan, Amanda turned her head to Thorn. Her gaze connected with his.

Something twisted in the pit of Thorn's stomach, and a startling thought blazed through his mind. *I want to have babies with this woman.* In that moment, he wanted it more than anything. Amanda was his future. He knew it. But did she feel the same way? Even if she did, she may not want to have kids. Hell, he hadn't thought he wanted any himself. Not until Ryan and Reagan came into the picture and he realized how great babies were.

And, of course, not until Amanda.

She sat back.

"How are you doing?" he asked softly.

"Okay. Having these four here has helped a lot." She lowered her voice. "Has he been found yet?"

"No, but I'm doing everything I can."

She laid her hand on his leg. "I know you are."

"Do you know if he knows anyone in Florida? Anyone he could be staying with?"

She shook her head. "I came to Florida because neither of us had any ties here."

"Have you seen a specific car following you or hanging around your neighborhood recently?"

Her face flushed. "No."

He put his hand over hers. "He may not be following you. I'm trying to find any lead on him. That's all."

"Hello," a man's voice called out.

Thorn flinched, and his hand automatically went to his sidearm.

"Pizza delivery," the man added.

Beth stood with her purse in her hand. "I'll take care of it."

Thorn lifted his hand from his firearm slowly, hoping Amanda hadn't noticed.

A minute later, Beth returned with two pizza boxes. "Who's hungry?"

Thorn stayed for as long as he could, but lunch breaks always flew by. Amanda walked him down to his car, and he caught how she peered left and right along the road, searching for Damon. He had looked, too, but no one else was around. At the driver's side door, Amanda looped her arms around him and pressed her mouth to his. Out in the open. With strange men walking up and down her driveway. With Damon potentially watching, seething.

Thorn framed her face with his hands and deepened the kiss. She responded right away. Her lips closed around his, lightly sucking. First his top lip, then she switched to his bottom lip, giving him the opportunity to enjoy her bottom and top lips one at a time, too. He slid one of his hands to her neck. The pad of his index finger settled over her pulse. As they kissed, he felt every beat of her heart and how it pounded harder when his tongue licked her lips. She opened her mouth for him, and their tongues caressed. Her pulse raced beneath his finger. He leaned in closer, and her pulse skipped a beat. It leapt a second later, hitting his finger with erotic power. That had him reining in his own libido. Although it took everything he had in him to stop kissing her, he gradually edged away from her addictive lips.

"I hate leaving you with *him* out there," Thorn said with his forehead against hers.

"Me, too."

"I'll call you later. Okay?"

She nodded. "Drive carefully."

He smiled. "I will. Bye."

"Bye." Still, she pulled away from him reluctantly.

In the driver's seat, he turned on the ignition, but he waited until she was back inside the house before driving away. He went to The Fighting Chance and searched the front and back parking lots for Damon. Beth had said Damon came from the side where the picnic table sat beneath a cluster of palm trees, so Thorn went over there. His gaze searched the ground for foot prints, but the grass grew thickly. On top of the picnic table, stubbed out in the wood surface, was a pile of cigarillos with the plastic tips attached. Many people sat at this bench, from groups of teenagers to mothers with strollers.

Thorn eyed the patch of woods beside the bench. He walked into the pine tree-shaded spot. Pine needles cushioned his steps. A group of palmetto bushes grew several feet within the small section of woods. He inched closer, with his hand resting on his sidearm. When he came around it, he found a collection of black beer bottles.

His brows lowered. He faced the parking lot. From where he stood, he could see the parking lot and the windows for The Fighting Chance.

He took out his cell phone and sent a text to Amanda. *Can you tell me about a few of his habits? Like what beer he drank and if he smoked?*

The three dots appeared as Amanda typed out a response. *He always drank Guinness Draught and smoked Black & Milds.*

Thorn nudged one of the bottles on the ground to see the label—Guinness Draught.

"Son of a bitch."

Another text came in. *Is something wrong?*

He debated whether or not to tell her. She should know, but he didn't want to give her the news through a text message.

No. Everything is okay.

He hated telling her that. There wasn't anything okay about this. Damon had been lurking outside The Fighting Chance for who knew how long, spying on Amanda, Beth, April, all of them. Damon knew who was close to her. He'd seen Thorn with her. Several times.

Thorn snapped pictures of the beer bottles, cigarillos, the palmetto bushes, and the bench, along with the views each offered of The Fighting Chance. Then, with gloves on, he collected the cigarillos into an evidence bag. In another evidence bag, he stashed the beer bottles. After going through Amanda's and Damon's records, he knew about the evidence collected from Amanda whenever she went into the hospital. When he had stabbed her, he'd been arrested. They had his fingerprints, as well as his DNA. The crime lab would be able to run the cigarillos and the beer bottles for prints and traces of saliva to see if they matched Damon. And they would. It was too much of a coincidence.

Back at the department, he dropped off the evidence and got back to work trying to figure out where Damon hid. He didn't think Damon slept in the woods beside The Fighting Chance, but he could be that desperate. Amanda said he'd fled on foot when the sirens got too close, and she hadn't heard a car speeding off. Could he be hiding in the woods around her house? That could be why they hadn't caught him fleeing. He could be out there right now, watching the front door being repaired.

Lying in wait.

Thorn got permission from Chief Cormac to search the woods around Amanda's house. On the street behind her house, he parked his car so they wouldn't see him. There was a lot of untouched Florida wilderness directly behind her house, giving Damon prime real estate to stalk her. With his gun in his hands,

Thorn tramped carefully through the woods. Up and down, he walked the grid in the same fashion forensic investigators used while scouring a crime scene. He scrutinized every square inch. Ears and eyes peeled, he worked methodically. His shoulders grew tired from holding his gun at-the-ready, aimed at the ground in front of his feet, and he became thirsty, but he pushed all that aside.

Halfway through the grid, he found a black bottle. He clenched his jaw as he crouched down. With his gun back in its holster, he slipped on a single glove and rolled the bottle around.

Sure enough, it was a Guinness Draught. He took a picture of it and placed a red flag there so he could come back and bag it later. Then he continued on.

Up and down.

Up and down.

He didn't pause again until he reached the edge of the lot. That single bottle was the one thing he'd found. Not much, but it placed Damon there. He could've been drinking in the woods, waiting for the nighttime hours to crawl by before he could creep out and bust down Amanda's door. Thorn doubted it had been the first beer he'd drunk. Not just the one he'd taken from Amanda's fridge, either. He could've had a case, downing one after the other. When he ran, he might've grabbed the cardboard case full of empty bottles and dropped one in his haste.

Thorn bagged the single bottle and looked toward Amanda's house. Damon would've had an excellent view of the back of her house, been able to see the light in Amanda's bedroom turn off. Then, under the cover of darkness, he could've snuck into her backyard and around her house to the front door. The fact Thorn had been sneaking around in the same woods without Amanda knowing didn't make him feel right, but this was his job. He'd do whatever it took to catch Damon.

Burnett met him at the department. "Did you really find bottles of Damon's preferred beer in the woods where Amanda works?"

Thorn held up the bag he held. "And one in the trees directly behind her house."

Burnett eyed it with the same disgust Thorn felt. "She's not safe."

"I know."

"He got close last night. That will make him want to escalate things. He could make another attempt tonight."

Thorn continued marching toward the crime lab. "I know."

Burnett followed him. "Is she going to be home tonight?"

"I don't know."

"I'll talk to Cormac and volunteer to be a car guarding her house tonight."

Thorn stopped and looked at his friend. "You don't have to do that."

"You're a part of my family." He indicated around at the department. "And you love her, so that makes her a part of my family, too. I have your back."

"Thank you."

"We should have a car on her street to watch the front and one on the street behind to watch the back. I'll ask Davis to see if he'd mind being the second car. Unless you want to do it…"

Thorn stilled. If Amanda wanted to stay home

tonight, he'd want to be *inside* the house with her, not outside of it. If Damon got in, Thorn wanted to be there like a fucking attack dog. Except, he couldn't make a decision like that for Amanda. "Ask Davis, and I'll let you know what we'll do tonight before I clock out."

"Okay. And I'll say it again, I've got your back." He clapped Thorn on the back for emphasis. "And I've got hers."

"I appreciate that."

Thorn did whatever he could think of while waiting for his work hours to run out. He checked traffic camera videos at the intersection near The Fighting Chance for the day Damon had come in looking for Amanda, but Thorn didn't see his truck or catch a glimpse of Damon behind steering wheels coming or going. He could be utilizing ride-sharing services, so Thorn called around, asking if they could check their records for Damon Hunter, since many of these services required users to link to a social networking account and also collected payment through a valid credit card. But every service he called had no records of Damon Hunter. He must be doing his moving about on foot. Or in a car with heavily tinted windows. Either way, Thorn couldn't track his whereabouts. And since he hadn't called Amanda, Thorn had no way of pinpointing him that way.

Damon took his last name to heart. He was hunting Amanda and making sure that no one could turn him from the hunter into the hunted. But Thorn was the hunter with a badge. Finding criminals was what he did best.

With thirty minutes left of his shift, he called Amanda.

"Hey, Thorn."

"Hey, I have a question to ask you. Are you planning to stay at your house tonight?"

"I think so."

Thorn propped his elbow on his desk and leaned his temple against his fist. "Are you sure?"

"Yeah. He made me run before. I'm not going to let him do that again."

Thorn cursed inside.

"I have two questions for you now," she said.

"Okay."

"I'm ordering Chinese. Would you like to have dinner with me, and what do you like?"

Relief had him sinking back into his chair. "I would love to have dinner with you. I like pot stickers and chow mein."

"Great. I'll add that to my order. You're off in thirty minutes, right?"

"Yeah." A smile stretched his lips. He liked that she knew his hours.

"Then I'll see you soon."

"You will. Bye."

"Come hungry. Bye."

Thorn was starving. The pizza he'd consumed for lunch had long since been burned off from walking the grid, driving here and there, and making numerous calls. Not to mention how his anger and worry had been eating at him all day. Dinner with Amanda was exactly what he needed.

Chapter Twelve

Amanda placed an order for potstickers, chow mein, sweet and sour chicken, spring rolls, and spicy tofu. Beth and Donovan left to get their kiddos ready for bed. She was thankful for them spending the entire day with her. They helped her to forget about Damon, but they weren't strong enough to get Thorn off her mind. Where Damon used to tower over everything in her mind, Thorn now stood, strong but gentle. He filled her thoughts and her heart, and she wanted him to fill so much more.

She sat on the couch. Her legs bounced up and down nervously. She bit her bottom lip and glanced at her phone repeatedly. When a knock sounded on her new front door, she hopped to her feet. Her heart launched into her throat. She put her hands down at her sides to calm herself, and so she wouldn't run to the door.

"Relax," she whispered. "Relax."

She checked through the peephole first. Then, hoping he wouldn't be able to see her nerves with his detective eyes, she opened the door. "Hey." She stepped aside to let him in. As he did, she caught sight of a cop car sitting out front. "Who is that?"

"Officer Burnett. He's a good friend of mine."

Officer Burnett caught her staring and waved.

She waved back. "So…cop presence is necessary?"

In the doorway, inches from her, he met her eye. “Yes.” He took her hand. “Let’s go inside. I’ll tell you about it more.”

Did Thorn suspect Damon to be close and didn’t want him to see them? She quickly shut and locked the door. This time, she had one dead bolt and chain.

Thorn led her to the couch and sat down. She took the cushion beside him. “What’s going on?”

“I found Black & Milds on the picnic bench beside The Fighting Chance. And in the woods right there I found Guinness Draught bottles.”

Her breathing quickened.

“Then I came here and canvassed the woods behind your house. I found another Guinness Draught in a spot with a perfect view of your backyard and bedroom window. His black Ram wasn’t seen anywhere last night. There are no records of him at any motels or hotels or bed and breakfasts within close proximity, and no ride-sharing services have records of him, either. I believe Damon has been moving around on foot and hiding out in the woods.”

She stared down at their joined hands. “That should surprise me, but it doesn’t. He’s the ultimate predator. He knows how to prey on women. Or…more precisely…he knows how to prey on me. It’s all he knows. He’s good at it.”

“I’m better at what I do. I guarantee you that.” The fierceness in Thorn’s eyes didn’t scare her as the fierceness in Damon’s eyes did, because there was a difference. Damon’s was insidious. Thorn’s was protective.

“I believe you,” she said while squeezing his hand. “I’m glad you’re here. And the food should be here any minute, too."

"I wanted to be here. Even if there wasn't any food."

"Even if I didn't have any food, I'd still want you to be here."

Thorn picked up their joined hands and kissed the back of hers.

The doorbell rang.

"I'll get it," he said and stood.

"Oh, wait. I have the tip in the kitchen."

"That's okay. I'll take care of it."

She got beers from the fridge, and he answered the door. Back in the living room, she set plates, forks, and napkins on the coffee table. Thorn came back carrying a to-go paper bag of Chinese food. Sitting side by side, they pulled out the containers.

"I'll repay you half the bill for the food," Thorn said.

"No, you don't have to. I asked you over for dinner."

"I want to." He took out the fortune cookies. "I also want to help cover half the repair costs for the doors."

She stopped with a container of white rice in her hands. "I can't let you do that. You didn't break them, and it's not your house."

He shifted toward her. "I know that, but…" He paused. "Can I call you my girlfriend?"

Heart pounding, she nodded.

"As my girlfriend, I don't want you to have to pay for all those repairs yourself. They don't come cheap, and I want to help out."

Silently, she tore off the top of the paper sleeve for

the chopsticks and pulled them out. "If that's what you want to do…"

"I do."

"Then, this once, I accept. Let's just hope he doesn't create any more costly damage."

Thorn laid his hand on her leg, and his thumb rubbed her jeans. The contact created ribbons of silky heat through her body. "I'm here to make sure he doesn't."

They ate dinner, passing the containers back and forth. Sometimes, they ate from the same container, and their chopsticks clicked together. Amanda laughed victoriously when she stole the potsticker he had been trying to pick up with his chopsticks. This wasn't something she'd experienced in the past. Back then, dinner had been fraught with anxiety.

Damon had expected food on the table when he got home from work. If it was late, he'd scream at her that she had one goddamn thing to do. If she had cooked him something he didn't like, he'd throw the food at her. Plate and all. If she burned something on accident, he'd slap her in the face. With Thorn, eating dinner was relaxed and fun—a time to bond, chat, flirt.

She cracked open her fortune cookie. "'Your happily-ever-after is coming.'"

Thorn pulled out the curl of paper from his broken fortune cookie. "'Stay on your path.'"

She picked at her nails. "Last year, Beth and I had a hibachi lunch and my fortune read, 'Give love a chance.'" She looked him in the eye, although her chest tightened and her heart thudded with excitement and fear. Fear because she had considered telling Thorn this many times before but had never had the guts. "I thought of you right away. I wanted to give love a chance, but I was scared. It sounds silly to admit that a fortune cookie helped me to be brave, but it did. Shortly after that was the Goldwyn Christmas party, when I had gathered enough courage to kiss you under that mistletoe." She smiled. "I've kept that fortune in my wallet as a reminder of how I can give love a chance. With you. And, apparently, my happily-ever-after is closer than I realize."

Thorn lifted his hand. His fingers stroked her jawline. "You make me happier than I have ever been."

She covered his hand with hers and closed her eyes. Never before had someone told her she made them happy. For Damon, she only ever inspired negative feelings in him—wrath, jealousy, possessiveness, and dangerous lust. Actually, the one time he appeared happy was after he'd abused her in bed for his own sexual appetite. He didn't know the meaning of intimacy. Or, rather, his meaning of intimacy was deranged and downright vile. She didn't know anything else. She took Thorn's hand. In her lap, she laced and unlaced her fingers with his. These weren't hands that had ever hurt her. These weren't hands that *would* ever hurt her. Before Thorn, she only knew hands that punched, dragged, slapped, choked, and stabbed.

"In a book I read a long time ago, the male character told the heroine he wasn't going to make love *to* her but rather that he was going to make love *with* her." She paused as her heart rate increased; she couldn't believe she was saying this, but she wanted to more than anything. "Up until that moment, I had no idea there was a difference between someone making love *to* you and someone making love *with* you. What Damon did, and every time he did it, he did it *to* me, not with me, and there wasn't any love in it at all. Not a drop. I don't know what that's like." She stared at Thorn now. "Can you show me?"

He blinked. "Show you…?"

She answered in a whisper. "What it's like to make love *with* someone."

His lips parted. He inhaled, filling his lungs. "Are you sure?"

She lowered her gaze as her stomach jittered, and she nodded.

He lifted her chin with his fingers. "My eyes…" His voice was little more than a breath.

Her gaze rose to meet his.

"I need to hear you say it."

She swallowed. "I'm sure. I want this. I want you."

Hearing that, Thorn inched to her, magnetized. He kissed her as if he'd never kissed her before and didn't want to stop. His lips savored hers. This was how a man kissed a woman he adored. This was how Thorn kissed her every time their lips touched. She released his hand and took his shoulders. Her lips worked with his, tasting and enjoying.

Delicious explosions burst throughout her system. While his right hand stayed beneath her chin, his other hand cupped the base of her head. When he tipped her head back gradually, she knew what he wanted. She opened her mouth, and their tongues met. She grasped his shoulders. Although their lips were interlocked, the rest of their bodies weren't touching. She scooted closer until their legs touched. Then she leaned into him so her breasts pressed into his solid chest.

He let out a groan, but his hands didn't move below her shoulders. For months, he'd been cautious with her, but she didn't want that anymore. Didn't require it. She craved his touch. Everywhere. She needed to learn what she'd been missing, what he could give her.

"Don't be afraid to touch me," she said into his mouth. "Please."

His hand at the back of her head lifted, and then he trailed the tips of his fingers from her neck down her back. She shivered against him and laughed.

He laughed, too.

She eased back enough to gaze into his eyes, but she didn't say anything. Instead, her hands slid along his shoulders to his neck, and she brought her mouth to his. As much as she wanted him to touch her, she wanted to touch him, too. Every plane, every muscle. She desired to get to know his body in a way she'd never acquainted herself with a man's body before.

After the trauma she'd endured for far too long, she hadn't wanted that and never thought she would again. Men had frightened her. Repulsed her. Sometimes the whiff of a specific note in a cologne sent her into a panic. At times, hearing a man's voice had made her body shut down. She'd avoid looking them in the eye and would even get out of line if one came up behind her, whose build made her feel threatened. And then Thorn came into her life. She hadn't had any of those reactions to his cologne, his voice, his presence. He was different. He was right.

He moved his lips to the spot beneath her ear. Kissing, sucking, and nibbling gently, he caused sensations that were foreign to her. Foreplay wasn't something she knew anything about. Damon had always been dangerously revved to go, whether she was prepared or not, mostly not, and his end goal was always his release. Never hers.

She slid her hands down his chest before wrapping them around his middle. As he paid attention to her earlobe, she ran her nails over his shirt. First down his back. Then across his ribs. Finally, along his lower back, following the top of his jeans to his hips. His moans excited her.

He kissed his way up her neck to her mouth, where he increased the pressure. With her hands on his hips, she pressed more firmly into him.

Clasping her hands, he drew her to her feet. "In your bedroom?"

She nodded and then remembered how he needed her to voice her wants. "Yes."

He led her to the bedroom, but halfway there, he halted and faced her. "We can't."

Her shoulders lowered. "Why not?"

He winced. "I don't have a condom on me." His fingers caressed the insides of her wrists. "I bought some, but I didn't want to carry any on me in case the universe thought I was trying to pressure you or push you before you were ready."

That had to have been the cutest thing she'd ever heard. His thoughtfulness touched her. She coiled her arms around his neck. "It's okay. I'm on the pill. It's never failed me before." Damon had never known she was on the pill. She hid them in a CD case in her car.

Thorn's hands settled on her hips. "It's more than pregnancy, though. Six months ago, I got a whole panel done to check for STDs and HIV. It came back negative, and I haven't been with another woman. I've only wanted to be with you, but we should wait until you can see the papers yourself."

His honesty and interest in her well-being had her pressing her mouth to his. She gave him a soft, sweet kiss. "I don't have to see them. I trust you," she said with their lips touching. Then she shifted back to meet his eyes. "I have papers, too. In my bedroom. All negative results. They're from back when I first moved here, though, but I haven't been with anyone since. I wasn't ready. Not until you."

Thorn's hands touched her cheeks, and he kissed her forehead. "I know. I don't need to see them, but there is something else I need to ask…" He gazed into her eyes. "Do you want me to pull out?"

That was something Damon had never asked her. He'd never used condoms, never pulled out, never gave her a choice. Hence the need to hide her birth control from him.

Thorn's question was an important one. In one situation, not pulling out could be intimate. In a vastly different situation, it could be sexual violence. She'd experienced the latter every time Damon had violated her. The former was what she wanted to experience now and with Thorn. Only Thorn.

"No." She stepped closer to him until their bodies bumped and she could feel his erection straining against his jeans. He squeezed his eyes shut. A groan rumbled in his throat. "I want all of you."

His eyelids flipped open. "Are you sure?"

Her heart raced, but in a good way. This was what she wanted to happen. This man. This intimacy. "Yes. And, please, no more questions."

He grinned. "Yes, ma'am."

She laughed as he led her the rest of the way to her bedroom. Once inside, she closed the door. Not out of fear, but to close them in this moment.

Thorn put his hand on the light switch. "Lights?"

She pulled his hand away from the switch and went to her bedside table where she tapped her touch lamp once. A warm glow lit the room. She wasn't ready to make love in blazing lights yet, but she also didn't want to be immersed in the darkness. She wanted to see Thorn. The bulb gave off enough light to keep her from panicking.

Still, her body quivered.

Thorn rubbed her arms. "That was a question, but this isn't. If I do something you don't like or don't want me to do, tell me right away. I'll stop. And if you change your mind at any point, please let me know. I won't be mad. I promise. You don't have to be scared to tell me to stop. Understand?"

"That's technically a question," she whispered with a shaky smile.

He dipped his chin. His gaze didn't shift from hers. "I need to know you understand that you can ask me to stop."

She ran her fingers down his cheek to his jaw. "I understand, and I need you to understand that, right now, I don't want you to stop."

Their lips came together. His kiss wasn't bruising or branding. It was accepting and giving. As they kissed, his fingertips skimmed down the underside of her arms all the way to the tips of her fingers. The ticklish contact of his fingers grazing her palms had her shivering against him again.

His lips curved against hers. “You keep doing that.”

“I’ll probably keep doing it.” What he did was brand new and felt amazing.

“I hope so. I like it.” He lifted one of her hands to his mouth. One at a time, he lightly sucked on the tips of her fingers. The entire time he did this, he held eye contact.

Her breathing hitched. When he picked up her other hand, he caught her by surprise when he flicked the tip of his tongue up the center of her palm with a feathery-light touch.

Another shiver.

This time, she got to see his grin.

He kissed the inside of her wrist so softly she barely felt it. Moving up her arm to her shoulder, the pressure of his lips on her skin increased. Then he angled her head to the side, the opposite side from before, and planted kisses along her throat. He touched the pulse point in her neck with the tip of his tongue and kept it there for several seconds. With the strong beats vibrating his tongue, and the erotic visions of what else his tongue could do, she pushed her hips into him. The contact had an explosion of wet heat blooming between her legs.

Thorn slipped his tongue into her mouth with a groan. He rocked against her, matching the motion of his tongue. A sound of pleasure she’d never heard come out of her mouth broke free. Startled, she took a step back. Her body trembled with passion.

“I’m sorry,” Thorn panted. “I shouldn’t have—”

She shook her head. “No.” She caught his hands when he made as if to retreat. “I’m feeling things I’ve never felt before. I'm okay."

To prove it, she resumed her position. Her hands flattened against his chest, and she ran her palms down to his abdomen, feeling him through the cotton fibers of his shirt. She took her time, enjoying the blind journey, not knowing if she'd feel a dip from his abs or the cuts in his torso or the defined, raised muscles. When she reached the hem of his shirt, she slipped her hands beneath it to feel his skin. For a moment, she explored him this way, with her hands beneath his shirt, crawling up farther and farther. She found his chest and teased his nipples. Finally, she wanted to see what she touched. She took his shirt in her hands and began to pull it up his body. He helped her to strip him of his shirt. Once bare, her gaze roamed over him. Heat scorched her inside and out. Her face burned with it, but she wanted that burn.

She brought her lips to his chest. His skin was so hot against her lips she thought she'd burst into flames. On fire with desire, she made a path of kisses from shoulder to shoulder. Traces of soap, the unique scent of his skin, and a hint of cologne teased her nostrils and intoxicated her senses. She licked the trench between his pecs. Then she skimmed her fingernails down the middle of his stomach to his navel. His abdomen squirmed at her touch.

Thorn's hands came to her hips, as if he needed to be steadied. He put his forehead to hers, and she sensed him reining himself in. Then his hands inched up, raising her shirt. Cool air touched the sensitive skin of her scar, and she caught his hands.

She gasped. "Wait."

"You don't have to take it off."

She pressed her lips to his. “Wait.” She lowered her forehead to his shoulder and breathed in and out. Her abdomen was something she’d protected ever since Damon had sliced her open. No one else had ever touched her scar. And although she’d shown it to Thorn once already, her scar had never been as naked in front of someone else as she was about to be with Thorn.

Thorn didn’t push her. He didn’t speak. His hands stroked her back as she continued to breathe in and out.

Slowly, she extracted herself from his arms and turned her back to him. “Okay.”

His fingers pinched the hem of her shirt. He drew it past her head, and she slipped her arms out of it. Then she reached behind her. Her hands found the rough fabric of his jeans. With her hands on his hips, she pulled him in. His chest met her bare back. His own hands came to her hips as their bodies brushed. For a moment, they stood like that while she attempted to settle her quaking system. Except, nothing could slow down her heart rate. Not with Thorn’s body against hers. Not with her own lust roaring through her veins.

She took the hand he had placed on her right hip, and, using her fingers to guide his, she put the pad of his finger on the end of her scar. Turning her head into the side of his neck, she held her breath and trailed his finger along her scar. He’d be able to feel the smooth skin as well as the jaggedness of the tissue beneath that from her flesh being pulled together with sutures. She squeezed her eyelids shut. Her body tensed, her core became rock-solid, and her other hand gripped the denim over Thorn’s thigh. The scar was less than six inches long, but the memory and turmoil it brought was far bigger than that. Thorn didn’t move at all, letting her share her scar with him at her own pace. At the end of it, she exhaled and released her strangled hold on his jeans.

Thorn laid his palm on her scar. His other hand crossed in front of her and curled around her jaw. He turned her head and kissed her passionately. Her head spun.

She rotated and threw her arms around him. The heat they created magnified tenfold. His hands caressed her back. Everything he did electrified her. Between their bodies, she worked on his belt. Once the metal prongs freed the leather, she pulled the belt from the loops. The leather retained Thorn's body heat, the inside layer had been worn down from use, and the roughness sent a memory she'd long buried to the front of her mind.

Damon had fitted a belt from his own pants around her neck, even as she cried and pleaded for him to stop. He didn't. He tightened the belt until it choked her. Then he used it to yank her around on the bed, treating her like a dog. He forced her onto her hands and knees and took his place behind her. Whenever he wanted a reaction out of her, he tugged on the belt. He forced her head back so far she couldn't breathe. She bore the marks on her neck for weeks.

She dropped Thorn's belt. The buckle struck the floor with a smack. She held still and closed her eyes to count to ten.

Thorn backed away. "Amanda, what is it?"

"Flashback," she managed.

She opened her eyes to see him staring down at the floor.

"My belt did that?"

She nodded.

Horror filled his face. “I won’t wear one ever again if it’s a problem.”

She clasped her hands around one of his. “That’s not necessary. It’s gone.”

He considered her. “Are you okay?”

“Yeah.” She glanced at her bed. “I’m ready.”

So he knew she meant it, she crawled onto the bed. Seconds later, he stretched out beside her and held her close. They kissed for several minutes, building back up to where she’d been before she crashed down thanks to that flashback.

Finally, Thorn began to investigate the rest of her body with his lips. He kissed her chest and cleavage, following the outline of her bra, and made his way down her stomach. When he reached her scar, he paused. She watched him inspect it up close. Her insides twisted. She had the urge to cover it, but she wrapped her hands in the bedcover, because she wanted Thorn to see all of her, even the shadows of what Damon had done.

He lowered, and his lips brushed ever-so-softly against her scar. The touch had her hands clenching into fists. Not from pain but from the staggering amount of love she felt pouring forth from his lips.

Lifting onto his knees, he stared down at her. His fingers came to the button of her jeans.

“May I?”

“Yes.”

Taking his time, he popped loose the button, pulled down the zipper, and drew her pants down her legs. At the foot of the bed, he took the briefest of moments to admire her. Before she could shrink in embarrassment, he knelt on the bed again. But he didn't return to her. He bent over and kissed her ankle. One kiss after the other, he lavished attention on her shin and thigh. When he reached the apex of her leg, he shifted to the other. This time, working his way down. All the while, his hands massaged her leg. His fingers grazed the back of her knee, causing her to shiver once more.

Thorn smiled. "I was waiting for that to happen again."

She couldn't respond before he went back to it, finishing his task with a kiss to her ankle.

He came back and pulled her into a sitting position. His arms came around her, and his fingers started to unhook her bra clasp. She jolted. Her hand covered her left cup where Thorn's business card was tucked into a slit in the silk.

"I…I don't take it off in case I need your card."

Thorn framed her face and gazed into her eyes. "I'm here. Right here, and I'm not going anywhere." He kissed her between her brows. "But you can keep it on if it makes you comfortable."

She mulled over his words. He was right there. If she needed him, she wouldn't have to call him, wouldn't have to remember his phone number in case of an emergency. His promise to not leave her repeated in her mind, aware he wasn't lying. He was there, and he'd continue to be there. "No, you're right. I don't need it." She lowered her hand. "Go ahead."

He didn't ask her if she was sure. For that she was glad, because it meant he no longer second-guessed her. He unhooked her bra and drew the straps down her arms. Goosebumps spread over her breasts. He didn't toss her bra carelessly away as most men did but set her bra aside, respecting what it meant to her. In a way, it was a connection they had. His business card had been the first stage of their relationship.

Staring into her eyes, Thorn's hands slid up her ribs. His thumbs rubbed the sides of her breasts. She bit her bottom lip. "You're going to make me shiver again."

Grinning, he skated his fingers along the underside of her breasts, and she did quiver with delicious chills. Then he dipped his head, taking her into his mouth. A gasp flew from her vocal cords. He used his lips and tongue on her. Everything he did had the throb between her legs pulsating harder and faster. She said his name, and his mouth left her breast. Holding her in his arms, he laid her down on the bed.

Her body hummed beneath his. The frequency rose when his fingers trailed up her inner thighs from her knees. Her leg muscles convulsed. He curled his fingers beneath the sides of her underwear and pulled it to her feet. She trembled atop the bed, stark naked, and watched as Thorn stripped out of his jeans and boxers. The beauty of his body struck her in a good way. His masculinity wasn't menacing but alluring.

He positioned himself over her but turned her so they lay on their sides, face to face. The change relieved her. Damon had always smothered her on top with his full weight, stealing her breath and making her feel trapped. Thankfully, Thorn had the foresight to anticipate that.

"You're shaking," he said and embraced her.

"All good," she whispered and hooked her leg over his hip. "I swear."

His erection nudged at her body. "Ready?"

"Yes."

Gazing into her eyes, he entered her. His movements were gentle, intensifying the pleasure rippling through her body. She rocked her hips, matching his movements, bringing them closer and him deeper. Clutching his shoulders, she settled her head in the crook of his neck. Their moans mingled.

Thorn didn't increase the tempo or hurt her in any way. Their lovemaking stayed slow and sweet; everything she had expected from him and like nothing she had ever experienced before. Sensations stacked one on top of the other, building and building. Small cries escaped her. She dug her nails into him as she came excruciatingly close to climax. When she did, she called out her release like never before. She shuddered with the aftermath of it.

Thorn began to pull out. She knew what he was doing, so she flexed her leg muscles and pulled him back. That single action had him erupting.

Chapter Thirteen

They lay connected for several minutes, panting and waiting for their hearts to calm. The orgasm Amanda had continued to convulse throughout her body, so Thorn cuddled her to his chest and soothed her with his hands. Her tremors ceased eventually, and Thorn eased away. Seeing tears on her cheeks plunged his heart to his colon.

He reached out to her. "Did I do something wrong?"

"No, you were wonderful." She swiped at her cheeks. "These are good. I…I never knew it could be like that. I'm happy, but I'm also sad for myself…for not knowing it could be that way." She linked her fingers with his. "Thank you."

He kissed her fingers. "Thank *you*." She'd given him something she hadn't been comfortable in giving another man since Damon. He wanted her to know he valued her intimacy and what it meant for the two of them.

They stayed in bed for a while, with her head resting on his shoulder and his fingers playing with the locks of her hair, just talking and breathing and being. This felt amazing. Thorn didn't want it to end. He'd waited so long for this. Now that it happened, he couldn't believe it. He worried that if he moved, he'd wake up and find that he'd dreamt months into the future.

Amanda rose onto her elbow, and he stiffened, waiting for his dream to end. She stared down at him. "I thought you might've fallen asleep."

He risked shaking his head and lifted his hand to touch her cheek. "Just trying to stay in this moment for as long as possible."

Her hair curtained around them when she kissed him. He wanted to tell her right then that he loved her, but making love and saying it were two different things, so he bit his tongue.

She pushed back up. "Are you hungry? Thirsty?"

He smiled. "Both."

"Me, too."

"Can I use your bathroom?"

"Of course. I'll go reheat some of the food."

Thorn slipped on his boxers and went into the bathroom. He faced the shattered mirror. All other signs of Damon's intrusion had been wiped from the house, but this remained. It was a harsh reminder Damon was out there. Somewhere. Probably closer than Thorn liked.

Wearing his jeans, he left the bedroom. Amanda wore a short, terrycloth robe as she pulled down the blinds in the kitchen and pushed the plastic pieces to hide any gaps. She whirled around when he entered the kitchen.

"I'm sorry. I didn't mean to scare you."

"It's okay. I saw the blinds up in here and realized that my windows had been open all day. I want to double check to make sure everything is locked up tight."

"I'll help."

They went window to window, lowering blinds and flipping the locks. Then they consumed leftover Chinese food on the couch. Afterward, Amanda leaned against the couch's armrest and sat with her legs tented over his lap and her feet on the other side of him. Her proximity fed his libido. He skimmed his fingers from her knee to her ankle and back again. She laid her head against the couch cushion. Her eyelids drifted shut.

"You do like to make me shiver," she said.

"Yes, I do." He grazed his fingers higher up to her hip.

She peered at him from beneath her lashes. "Shouldn't you be getting some sleep for work tomorrow?"

"I'm actually off tomorrow."

"Really?"

"Mm-hm." He reached around and trailed his fingers up the back of her thigh.

She bit her lip, one of her sensual tics he also thoroughly enjoyed. "It's late now, but in the morning, I can see if Beth will give me the day off. Then we'll be able to spend the day together, sleeping in, eating whenever we want, having sex whenever we want…" She blushed. "And, of course, we can live stream movies and chill."

He smiled. "Sounds like the perfect day with you."

Later, Amanda came to life in her bedroom. She experimented with her level of intimacy and with him. At first, her hands were shaky, her kisses tentative, and her touches curious. It didn't take long for her to become confident, though. She tasted and kissed him between his shoulder blades and followed his spine, down his throat, and along his chest. She tickled and felt the differing textures of his skin from his arms to his happy trail. Her exploration increased his appetite times one thousand. His body vibrated. He wanted her more than ever, but he didn't dare take over.

Wearing the terrycloth robe, she straddled him. With her hands on his shoulders, she sank onto him. His hips reared up, and she half gasped, half moaned. Staring into his eyes, she peeled the robe from her shoulders. Underneath, she wore her bra out of habit, and he enjoyed the sight of it. He held her hips to feel her body gyrate against his. Her pace began slow and then escalated as she rode her desires. She moved her hands from his shoulders to his waist, and then, finally, to his thighs when she arched her back while racing toward climax.

Thorn held back until she detonated. Then she melted on top of him. Her adorable question moments later had him chuckling. "Did I do that right?"

"Baby, you were amazing."

****

In the morning, Thorn crept out of bed, not wanting to wake Amanda. He mixed up pancake batter in the kitchen while reminiscing over the night. His lips quirked. She was amazing—her openness and generosity, her fragility and strength. What she gave him that night, more than once, meant the world to him.

"You didn't have to get up to make breakfast." Amanda stepped up beside him.

He flipped a set of pancakes on a griddle. "I wanted to."

"Smells good. A man has never cooked for me before."

"I like to cook," he admitted. "I don't often have

the time to do it, but for you, I'll find the time." He was determined to give her all the things she'd never had and deserved.

Once the pancakes were consumed, Amanda called Beth to ask for the day off. "Hey, Beth. No, everything is fine, and I can't wait for the day when I call and you don't assume that something is wrong. Thorn's here. He took good care of me last night." She pressed her lips together. "What do you mean what do I mean by that?"

Thorn ducked his head toward his coffee cup to hide his grin.

"I'm not answering that. Nope. No. Nope. Don't you dare put Donovan on the phone!"

Thorn looked up. *Donovan better not get on the phone.*

Amanda laughed. "Okay. I called because I have a question. Would it be possible for me to take today off? I don't want to put you and April out." She listened silently a moment. "All righty then. I'm going to hang up now." She set down her phone and put her hands to her face.

"What'd she say? 'Hell no, get your butt to work?'"

"Actually, she gave me the day off, and then she said to enjoy the day with you. I guess she knows you have the day off, too."

"She would know my schedule."

"That wasn't so bad, but then Donovan shouted in the background, 'Safety first, kids.' I have a feeling we're not fooling them."

"Probably not."

"That's okay. I'm not trying to hide it from them. I tend to keep things close, especially my emotions."

He took her hand. "You had to."

She nodded.

"But you don't have to anymore."

She got up, walked around the table, and looped her arms around his neck. "You're helping me to learn that."

He held her. "It's my honor."

She smiled and glanced down at his jeans. "The next time you come over, you should bring some of your things. We might have to leave the house to get clean clothes."

"I have a duffel of stuff in my car. I packed it and kept it in my back seat in case you ever needed me, at any time."

"You did that?"

"Of course."

He slipped on his shirt and headed out to his car to retrieve his duffel bag. Burnett exited his car as Thorn walked down the driveway. "Hey," Burnett said. "I was about to leave. Do you want me to call in replacements for the day?"

"No, that's okay. I'm going to stay with her today."

Burnett nodded slowly. "And you stayed all night."

Thorn eyed him. "Not a word."

"No other words coming out of my mouth. See you later." He saluted Thorn and went back to his car. A moment later, he drove off.

Thorn brought his duffel bag inside.

Amanda played with the ties to her robe. "So…shower for two?"

Thorn nearly dropped his bag. "Hell ya."

The two of them spent the day as they had discussed, eating whenever they were hungry, relaxing on the couch, indulging in each other, and chatting about anything and everything. On the couch, Amanda lay between Thorn's legs, with her back against his chest. The TV was off. Music played in the background. For a while they breathed together as one while listening to music.

Amanda ran her fingers through the hairs on Thorn's arm. "I feel as though I've been with you my entire life."

Her omission surprised him, because he felt the same way.

"The way I am with you and how I feel around you is unlike how I've felt with any man. Even before. I didn't think I'd ever get this way again. Frankly, it's a miracle. But I want you to know that survivors of sexual assault can regress. We can feel normal and loved and be able to love in return one day, even for a long period, and then all of a sudden revert at the drop of a dime for days or weeks. What we have right now is amazing, and always will be, but I may have moments where this may be tough for me. Not because of anything you'll do, but because that's the nature of being a survivor."

Thorn pressed a kiss to her temple. "I understand, baby, and I will be here for whatever ups and downs you may have. I'll help you through them. If you want me to hold you, give you a shoulder to cry on, or give you space, I'll do it."

She wrapped her arms around his. "Thank you."

"Anything for you." And he meant it.

That night, he fell asleep, thanking the universe for the woman who slept beside him.

Chapter Fourteen

Amanda stood on her doorstep, kissing Thorn in the early morning light. Neither of them wanted their spectacular day to end, but they had their lives outside of her house. Thorn couldn't ignore his duties, or his obligation to find Damon, and she looked forward to getting back into the studio after two days away. She couldn't wait to talk to Beth and April, who no doubt had been speculating over the details of her and Thorn's long sleepover.

Thorn ran a hand down her ponytail. "Do you want to get together tonight?"

"Yes." She bit her lip. "You have to get up early, so I can come to your place after work."

"Sounds good." He kissed her. "The day can't end fast enough."

"Then you should get to work now so it will." She smiled. "See you later."

She waved goodbye before heading back inside. Two hours remained before she needed to head off to work, so she lingered over breakfast while dark clouds gathered above. In her room, rain splattered against the window as she packed a bag to take to Thorn's. Along with her perfume and deodorant, she added extra clothes and underwear, plus a hairbrush and toothbrush to leave behind for future visits. Doing this filled her with excitement. Taking this next step with Thorn was an adventure. She didn't know where it'd take her, but she looked forward to it because Thorn would be there for each step.

Rain fell harder.

Thunder rumbled in the distance.

She set her bag on the couch and debated what to do for the next hour. Lounging on the couch, she opened the cover of a book. Not often in her home did she feel as though she could relax, but after the amazing day she'd had with Thorn, she felt more relaxed than ever. She couldn't even remember the last time she'd read for pleasure. Usually, while at home, she was on edge, alert, waiting for Damon's large shoe to drop, and oddly enough, when it had the other night, it broke the tether that kept her chained to her perpetual fear.

She'd been expecting it to happen for ages that now that it finally did, it didn't feel as powerful anymore. Maybe that was because the anxiety had been far bigger than reality. Maybe that was because she'd lived through the worst already and made it out stronger. Maybe that was because she had Thorn now. And Beth. And Donovan. And April. And Leighton. She had people who cared about her, who would fight for her and with her. She also had The Fighting Chance—a place she went to in the real world and a place that dwelled inside her.

She read a couple of chapters before slipping a bookmark into place. Wind pelted rain into the windows as she headed toward her bedroom to get her things. In her hand, her phone beeped with a weather warning. She paused in the hallway and checked the screen to see the words *Tornado Warning*.

Her eyes widened. She entered in her passcode and opened the app to read the details. Her heart rate picked up when she read the warning was for her county. More specifically, it pinpointed the main road a block away from her street. Mouth dry, she scanned for more details. A tornado had been spotted in the southwest section of town, where she lived, moving northeast. Her hand shook as she watched the red cone of danger on the weather map showing the tornado to be heading toward her, not away. Even more frightening, they predicted it to be an EF3 on the Enhanced Fujita scale.

In her closet, she had a small mattress fit for a baby's crib. Fastened around it were a few leather belts, so she could hold the mattress over her while hiding in the bathtub. With that warning, she wouldn't take any chances. It was time to climb into the bathtub and put the mattress over her head. She was hurrying to her bedroom when the sound of glass shattering stopped her in her tracks.

Oh my gosh. It's here.

She raced toward where the sound had come from—the kitchen. Wind blew through her house, swaying a couple of pictures on the walls and rattling the horizontal blinds in front of the sliding glass door. She turned into the kitchen and froze. Damon stood there, dripping wet. For a split second, she didn't believe he was there. How could he be? It's daytime. He wouldn't commit a crime in broad daylight, would he? Then again, the storm was the perfect cover.

He took a step, breaking her shocked paralysis.

She shot toward her bedroom. As she ran, she stuffed her phone into her bra. Behind her, Damon gave chase. His boots pounded against the floor.

She sped into her bedroom and grabbed the door. As she went to slam it, she caught sight of Damon a few strides behind. She wouldn't be able to close and lock the door in time, so she spun around and shoved her back into the wood. Damon bulldozed into it, forcing her forward a step, but she dug in her heels. On the other side, Damon pushed. She pushed back. Then he rammed his shoulder into it, knocking her farther. She applied her muscles into shoving against his efforts, but he was stronger. He hit the door again with such force that she launched forward and fell onto her hands and knees a few feet away.

Scrambling to her feet, she calculated ways of escape in her head. If she went into her bathroom, she wouldn't be able to close the door. And she'd be trapped. The bathroom was a good place to go to in a tornado, but not in an intruder situation if you couldn't bar the door. So, she sprang onto the bed, hoping to make it across to her bedroom window. Damon caught her left ankle, and she dropped onto the bed. He had done so much to her on the bed they'd once shared—so many devastating, degrading things. But not here. Not this bed! Without missing a beat, she twisted around and slammed the bottom of her right sneaker into his face. His nose crunched. The break vibrated through her sole.

As he covered his bleeding nose with his hands, she rolled out of the way and fell to the ground. Her knees struck the floor hard, but she bounced onto her feet and dashed out of her bedroom for the front door.

In the living room, Damon tackled her. Her chin rapped against the floor, causing her teeth to snap together. He wrestled her onto her back, and then his hands closed around her throat. Squeezing. And squeezing. And squeezing. Unable to suck in a breath, she did exactly what she had been trained to do—what she had helped train others to do—she hooked her left leg around his and shoved off the floor. The maneuver caught Damon by surprise. She broke his hold on her neck and switched their positions successfully. Then she threw down her fist, cracking it into his face.

One thing she had learned was to never pause, always keep moving. So, she leapt to her feet to flee, but Damon swept her legs out from under her.

She got onto her knees and faced Damon to counter his next move. Except, he pulled out a hunting knife from a holster at his ankle. It was the same one he had stabbed her with before. Fear ping-ponged inside her. She could feel the blade piercing her as it had then. The pain. The searing burn. The warmth of her blood.

She rose to her feet but stayed crouched, ready.

Across from her, Damon brandished the knife. "If I can't have you, no man will."

He pounced.

She dodged and skirted around the coffee table to put distance between them. He stepped up to the coffee table on the other side.

"So, you know how to hit now." He sneered, even as blood drizzled from his nose, dripping off his beard and coating his neck. "That's not going to save you." He flashed the blade at her.

She picked up a throw pillow from the couch and held it in front of her, like a shield. Damon laughed at her pitiful attempt to protect herself. When he inched around the coffee table, she shifted her body, but she didn't retreat.

Amanda wanted him to get closer. Close enough to make a move. He towered over one corner of the coffee table, and she stood behind the adjacent corner. Although she appeared calm on the outside, on the inside, she quaked. She'd always known he was capable of killing her. His love had pushed him to stalk her, and that same demented love, that obsession, would drive him to commit murder.

Damon jabbed the knife at her stomach. At the same time, she thrust the pillow. The blade sliced through its cotton and poked through the other side. Gripping the pillow's edges, she wrenched it, forcing Damon's wrist to turn until he had to release his hold. She yanked the knife free and dropped the pillow. Then she lunged low.

The knife sank into Damon's thigh.

He let out a howl.

She wrenched the knife in his flesh before she tugged it out; twisting a blade once it was deep in flesh would keep the wound from closing.

With the knife clutched in her hand, she slipped away from the coffee table and ran to the garage. She slammed the door behind her and hit the button to lift the garage door. Wind blew through the crack. As the gap widened, more wind rushed in and plowed into the empty boxes she had set up on the right side of her garage. She jabbed the button two more times to get the door to lower. With the tornado threat, she couldn't go outside. It was too dangerous.

But…inside wasn't any safer. At least inside, she had a chance against Damon. Mother Nature was an opponent that shouldn't be challenged.

She hurried around the stacks of smaller boxes to

the refrigerator box set up against the wall. She pulled open the front cardboard piece and stepped inside. With hands covered in Damon's blood, she set the knife at her feet. Her fingers fumbled with her phone when she removed it from her bra. The screen lit up the dark space. She swiped her slick fingers over the screen to lower the glare. Trying to catch her breath, she brought up her texts and went to the last text she sent Thorn. Shaking, she tapped out a frantic message.

99111 Damonn

She sent it off, not caring about the typos. She had no time to fix them.

The door hit the wall when Damon propelled it open. She held her breath and clutched her phone to her chest. Through a pinpoint hole she had dug into the cardboard, she peeked out at him. He staggered over the floor, trailing blood that soaked his jeans.

Outside, the wind roared like a freight train.

Amanda swallowed. She'd heard enough stories about tornadoes to know they sounded like barreling trains. It really was coming. No cardboard box, no matter how big, would protect her from a tornado's feisty grip.

Upper lip sweating, she eyed Damon. In his hand, he held a switchblade. One knife apparently wasn't enough for him. Of course not. Not when it came to her.

The garage door banged with the gales blasting the house. The tornado was close. Too close. Staring through the peephole in the cardboard box, she watched Damon stumble to her car. He left behind a bloody handprint on the hood.

"Where are you, bitch? I know you're in here."

He peered through the driver's side window. It was

now or never.

Gripping her phone, she burst out of the box. He whirled around, and she plowed into him, slamming his back into the car door. With her hands on his shoulders, she rammed her knee between his legs. When he slumped forward, his arm swung out. The switchblade sliced through her shirt, cutting her across the abdomen. She let out a cry of pain as Damon collapsed onto his hands and knees. This was the opportunity she needed. She dashed for the garage door.

Damon shouted, “Get back here!”

She yanked the door shut behind her and locked it—the doorknob and the two deadbolts.

The house rattled.

While the walls vibrated, she ran to the opposite end of the house. In her bedroom, she closed the door and pushed her dresser in front of it. Although, she wasn’t sure what she was trying to keep out—Damon or the tornado? Or both? From her closet, she pulled out the crib mattress and hauled it into her bathroom. She shut the door, and her bedroom window shattered. Heart racing, she slid the wooden plank over the bathroom window. Then she tossed a towel into her bathtub. Her entire house shook, from floor to ceiling. She climbed into the bathtub, got down on her knees, and shifted the crib mattress onto her back. With one hand, she pressed the towel to her stomach to stop the bleeding, and with the other, she wrapped her fingers around the leather straps to keep the mattress in place.

An explosion of glass breaking echoed around her, mixing with the roar of wind and the groan of wood being ripped apart. Shampoo and conditioner bottles fell on top of her. Other items in her bathroom were swept off the counter and onto the floor. Wind tore apart the ceiling and set loose in her house. Plaster and wood pelted into the mattress. Amanda felt the vibration of the hits against her back.

Then the wind reversed, sucking everything up through the hole in the ceiling. It seized hold of the mattress protecting her and tried to yank it from her grasp. She let go of the towel to curl her other hand around the belts. The wind didn't release the mattress, though, but fought harder to take it from her. She applied all her strength in holding it, but it pounded her body as the sides flapped with the tornado's massive suction.

The blows stole her breath and battered the back of her head and spine. Her arm muscles burned. Her hands blistered from the leather straps. She let out a yell. Soon, she wouldn't be able to hold on anymore. Soon, she'd have to let go, but giving up wasn't her forte. She mustered the dregs of her buried strength. Her yell became a high-pitched scream. Her body lifted off the bottom of the porcelain tub.

Just when she thought it was over, that the tornado would suck her away, the wind dropped her, and debris buried her.

Chapter Fifteen

The 9-1-1 message from Amanda filled Thorn with the bitterest panic he'd ever felt in his life. He ran out of the police department. Outside, the sky was covered in thick, gray clouds that smothered the sun. Wind kicked up with force, tossing leaves and trash across the parking lot. He jumped into his car and started the ignition. The radio turned on and emitted an earsplitting alert. Following the noise, a weather bulletin followed.

"A tornado warning has been issued for Orange and Brevard County." What the bulletin said next added to Thorn's fear. A cell with the potential of developing into a tornado was located directly over where Beth and Donovan lived. With their luck, it wouldn't surprise him if the tornado touched down on their roof.

"Call Beth," he ordered the phone hooked up to his car.

"Calling Beth," the woman's robotic voice answered.

As the ringing filled his car, he sped toward Amanda's house.

A moment later, Beth answered.

"Beth, you guys need to take shelter now. There's a tornado cell above you."

"No. No, Thorn. That's an old report. There is a tornado, and it has touched down, but it's heading for Amanda. Not us."

Thorn stopped breathing. "What?"

"It's on her street!"

His heart sank to the pit of his stomach. Around the steering wheel, his hands broke into a cold sweat. He couldn't see the tornado through the trees lining the road he sped down, but he would be able to in a moment. The road ahead curved to the right, opening up to a view of the sky and landscape. With icy hands, he turned the wheel. His heart pounded as he followed the curve. Once he rounded it, his breath rushed out of him. The tornado was huge, a twisting, ferocious dark cloud of a beast feasting on the land. Not only land, but houses. Debris floated around the large, windy funnel. It moved slowly, devouring everything in its path, and Amanda was in its deadly path.

"It's big." His voice was no more than a whisper. "How can they get so big?"

"What do you mean 'it's big'? You can see it?" Her voice rose a few octaves. "How can you see it?"

Thorn stared at the tornado in sheer horror. That tornado was threatening the life of the woman he loved, but that wasn't all. He swallowed. "Because I'm heading to Amanda's now. She texted me. Damon is there."

"Oh my God."

Hearing the fear in Beth's voice increased his own.

"Amanda is smart," Beth added. "And she's strong."

"I know." His grip tightened on the steering wheel. "But she can't take on Damon *and* a tornado." As he raced down the road—the sole car heading toward the tornado—everything he ever wanted to tell Amanda blew through his mind. "I'm scared, Beth. I haven't told her I love her, yet, and I want to."

"You'll have a chance."

He shook his head. The closer he got to the tornado, the more massive it appeared. And it was right where Amanda lived, tearing apart her neighborhood, board for board.

"What if I don't make it in time?"

On the other end, Beth didn't answer his question.

Miles away, the tornado wreaked havoc. He'd never seen a tornado in real life, and he never wanted to see one again. Wind lashed at his car, causing it to swerve. He held on. Debris swept across the road. A tree branch hit the hood.

Horns blared as cars drove past him. He ignored them. Yes, he was headed for danger, and he wasn't going to stop.

"Thorn, please be careful." Beth's voice came from the speakers.

"I'll try my best."

"Call me when you find her."

"I will." He jabbed the "end call" button.

Less than a mile away, the tornado's structure started to break apart. The dark column expanded as it dissolved. Blue sky appeared through gaps of gray clouds. In moments, the tornado was nothing more than wisps of darkness. Even that evaporated into the atmosphere. Pieces of wood, roof shingles, insulation, and random objects drifted from the sky. Thorn dodged a kiddie pool when it collided into the road and rolled to the shoulder.

A couple of blocks from Amanda's house, the tornado's devastation came into view. The very ground was gone; the grass ripped up, leaving behind dirt. The trees left standing were bare. Others had fallen, exposing their large root bases. When he saw house after house flattened, his heart shattered. They were nothing more than rubble, spread far and wide. He wanted to stop and find survivors, but the woman he loved more than anything could be dead. He had to get to her.

Roads no longer existed. The tornado had stolen the street signs. Not a single thing resembled the old neighborhood. If he hadn't turned onto the street a second ago that led to her house, he wouldn't have been able to tell where he was.

He drove over the debris-covered road at a crawling pace, dodging around larger debris. His gaze searched left and right at the carnage. In minutes, the neighborhood had been laid to waste by Mother Nature. In minutes, peoples' lives had changed. In minutes, people may have died. He prayed Amanda was among the living, that the tornado hadn't won. That Damon hadn't won.

Every molecule of his body trembled with fear. He turned the car to see more of the same—the tornado's massacre. Amanda's house should be coming up on the left, but there were no houses on the left. There were no houses anywhere.

He eyed the rubble that went on and on, blending what used to be one house with the next. Then he caught sight of the back end of Amanda's car. The garage it had been parked in and the rest of the house had been demolished. His foot punched the brake pedal. He turned off the ignition and leapt out of his car.

"Amanda!" He worked his way up a heap of wood and concrete. "Amanda!" With his hands, he began tossing aside debris. "Amanda, can you hear me? Where are you?"

Please God, he prayed, *let her be alive. I can't lose her.*

He didn't know what he'd do if he found her and she wasn't alive. But he couldn't think about that now. She would be alive. He had to believe that.

"Amanda!"

He picked up a sheet of drywall. Underneath it were chunks of concrete. He threw them to the side to find more wreckage. Peering around, he couldn't believe what had become of her house, of the entire neighborhood. He didn't even know where to look for her, where to begin. She could be anywhere. She might not even be beneath this debris. The tornado could've picked her up. He'd heard about people getting sucked into a tornado and never being found again.

Dear God, please don't let that be the case for Amanda.

"Amanda, where are you?"

He thought he heard something.

"Amanda?"

Across the street, at another mountain of debris that had once been a house, someone searched for loved ones. That was the voice he had heard calling out. Not Amanda's.

Heart shaking along with his knees, he climbed over more trash to the heart of the heap. "Amanda…call out!"

"Here…"

He froze. "Amanda?"

"Thorn, I'm here!" Her muffled voice came from the corner where her bedroom used to be.

He hurried over and lifted a hunk of the roof from the top. Then he removed pieces of wood and insulation while digging through what was left of the ceiling. When he picked up a layer of drywall, he revealed a hole. Sunlight streamed through it, spotlighting Amanda. She knelt on top of a small mattress that partially covered the bathtub.

"Are you okay?" He dropped to his knees.

She nodded. "I think so."

He lowered onto his stomach. "Grab my hands."

She stood on the mattress and caught his hands. Straining, he hauled her up through the hole. She used her feet to gain leverage on the shambles that trapped her.

He rose onto his knees and lifted her higher. The second her upper body became visible, he wrapped an arm around her waist, then the other. She latched onto him. As he dragged her out, he lowered onto his back, pulling her on top of him. He made sure her legs were clear before embracing her.

"Thank God," he muttered and tightened his hold. "You're sure you're okay'?"

"Y-ycs." IIcr voicc shook.

"Come on." He drew her to her feet. "This is unstable. I need to get you down off this." Holding her hands, he guided her off the pile of rubble. On the ground, they stared at what had become of her home.

"Oh my God," Amanda whispered.

Thorn turned her away from the destruction and checked her out from head to toe. "No broken bones?"

"No."

He caught sight of the cut in her shirt and the blood. "You're bleeding."

"It's a scratch. I think it stopped."

"Can I see?"

She peeled the bloodied shirt from her abdomen. The cut was an inch above her scar. Trickles of blood continued to seep from it, but most of it had stopped as she said.

"He cut me with a switchblade."

Thorn's gaze snapped up. "Damon? Where is he?"

"I locked him in the garage."

He whirled toward where the back end of her car poked out of the demolished garage. "Stay here." He headed for it, climbing over drywall, furniture, and shingles. Anger built inside him as he chucked aside fractured two-by-fours and insulation.

A moan caught his attention. He followed it to a few feet away and lifted a flattened cardboard box, revealing a half-conscious man. Hands shaking, he uncovered the rest of the man's body and dragged him from the garage floor to his car. Damon moaned the entire way. Blood drenched his jeans. Cuts and bumps marred his skin, and Thorn didn't give a damn. He dropped the bastard onto the concrete. In the next second, he threw down his fist. His knuckles cracked into Damon's face, and it felt good. Then he removed his handcuffs, attached one cuff around Damon's left wrist, and the other around his car's grill.

"You're under arrest for a whole bunch of shit I don't have the time to list right now," he said and then went back to Amanda.

With Damon in his custody, the tornado gone, and Amanda in front of him, he couldn't hold back anymore. He tucked her close to his body, needing to reassure himself that he wasn't imagining her there. Her body against his felt wonderful—warm and soft. Alive. Every emotion he'd ever felt before welled up inside him.

"I love you," he whispered.

She leaned back to gaze into his eyes. "That's what I wanted to tell you."

The corners of his mouth lifted. "Beat you to it."

She smiled, too. "I love you, Thorn. I'm so happy I listened to that fortune cookie, and to my heart, and gave love a chance."

He cupped Amanda's face with his hands and stared deep into her eyes. "Thank God for fortune cookies."

She chuckled. "And for The Fighting Chance."

"Yes, definitely that."

A police car pulled up to them, and Burnett stepped out. "Donovan called me. Are the two of you okay?"

Thorn nodded. "Yeah, but can you deal with *that*?" He pointed at Damon, handcuffed to his grill and coming to with blood gushing down his face.

"Is that Damon Hunter?"

"Yes, it is."

"Damn. The tornado sure beat the shit out of him."

Amanda snorted.

Thorn smirked. "You don't mess with Mother Nature."

"Obviously not." Burnett started toward Damon. "I'll take him to the hospital under arrest and then personally see him locked behind bars."

"Thanks, man."

While Burnett hauled Damon to his feet and got him into the back of his police car, Thorn and Amanda kissed—in the middle of the tornado's aftermath, in each other's arms.

And they were right where they were supposed to be.

A word about the author…

Chrys Fey is the award-winning author of *Hurricane Crimes*, Book One of the Disaster Crimes Series, a unique concept blending romance, crimes, and disasters. She's partnered with the Insecure Writer's Support Group, running their Goodreads book club. She's also an editor for Dancing Lemur Press.

Fey lives in Florida and is always on the lookout for hurricanes.

~*~

Get *The Crime Before the Storm*, Donovan's FREE short story and prequel to *Hurricane Crimes*, by signing up for Chrys Fey's newsletter at:

http://bit.ly/2UlZjU0

Thank you for purchasing
this publication of The Wild Rose Press, Inc.

For questions or more information
contact us at
info@thewildrosepress.com.

The Wild Rose Press, Inc.
www.thewildrosepress.com

Amanda looked up from the current list of up-to-date payments for classes. A movement outside the glass storefront caught her eye. She tilted her head to see a man coming up the sidewalk from the side where the picnic bench sat. Through the vertical blinds, she glimpsed a square face—a short, rugged beard and long, dark hair pulled into a man bun. Her breath fled from her lungs. Her body went from icy cold to flaming hot in the span of a millisecond. She dropped to the floor and slid under the counter, beneath the ledge where they put their purses and cell phones.

"What—" Beth peeked at the windows. Then she snapped her fingers at April and pointed at the stools.

April jumped into action. She pushed the stools in so they blocked Amanda. The bell attached to the door jingled as April removed the jacket she wore and draped it across the stools, creating a curtain to shield Amanda.

From a crack, Amanda watched Beth move to stand in front of the twins, who were in their walkers playing peacefully. "I'm sorry, but we're going to be closing."

"I don't give a shit. I'm here for Amanda."

The sound of Damon's voice had her heart beating even harder. That voice had haunted her nightmares, had come back to life in her memories.

Beth cocked her head to the side. "Who? There's no one by that name here."

"Don't bullshit me. I know she works here."

His voice was closer now.

Praise for Chrys Fey

The Complete Disaster Crimes Series:
**The Crime Before the Storm*
(prequel, ft. Donovan)
Hurricane Crimes (#1)
Seismic Crimes (#2)
Lightning Crimes (#2.5, free story on Amazon)
Tsunami Crimes (#3)
Flaming Crimes (#4)
Frozen Crimes (#5)
A Fighting Chance (#6, spin-off, ft. Thorn)
The Disaster Curse (#7, ft. Thorn)

"THE DISASTER CRIMES SERIES has the potential to be a terrific series that is spell-binding and [will] have readers on the edge of their seats."

~InD'tale Magazine

~*~

*To get *The Crime Before the Storm*, Donovan's FREE short story and prequel to *Hurricane Crimes*, sign up for Chrys Fey's newsletter at:

http://bit.ly/2UlZjU0

www.ingramcontent.com/pod-product-compliance
Lightning Source LLC
Chambersburg PA
CBHW071313200626
46813CB00015B/1853